BOUND IN FLESH

AN ANTHOLOGY OF TRANS BODY HORROR

EDITED BY

LOR GISLASON

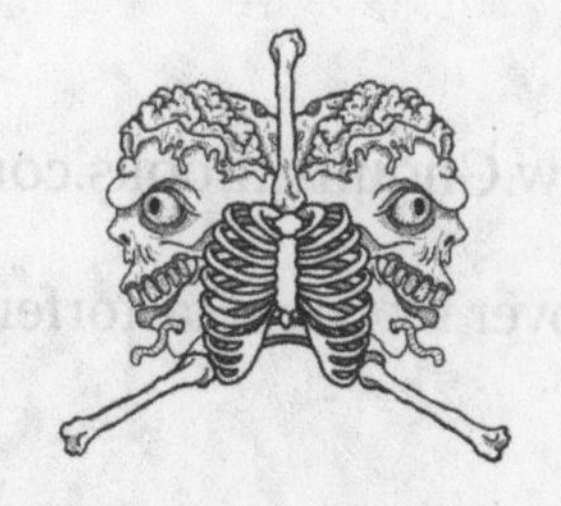

Ghoulish Books
an imprint of Perpetual Motion Machine Publishing
San Antonio, Texas

Bound in Fesh

ISBN: 978-1-943720-83-5

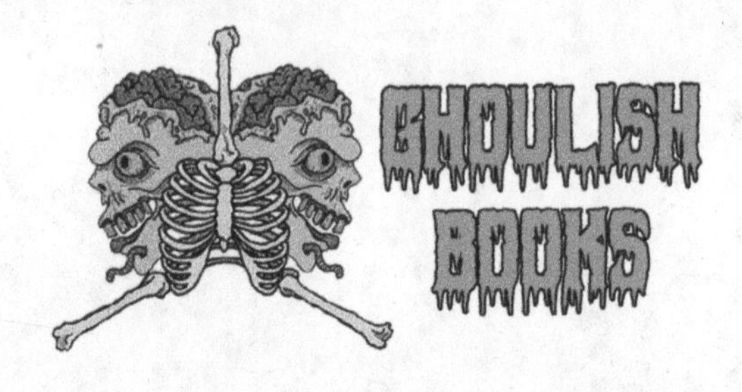

www.GhoulishBooks.com

Cover by Babs Rastorfer

TABLE OF CONTENTS

WHEN I POSTED a meme on Twitter alongside my desire for a body horror anthology penned by trans and non-binary authors, I could never have imagined it would lead to me editing a book. Then Max approached me with a very simple "ok, but what if that did exist?" Right now you are holding the result of that question—which was the fastest yes I've ever typed, by the way—the final group of stories that pushed their way into this world, naked and bloody and wonderful. Within these pages are months of work and love and I couldn't be prouder.

As trans individuals, you could say we have a leg-up on understanding the emotions (both good and bad) surrounding living in a body. The joy when someone affirms your identity and the frustration when you're denied that right. The violence we face just for being who we are. The way legislation (especially in the United States) denies people access to the care they need to live their lives. All of these things can be channelled into a story.

I'd like to thank Max for his guidance during this project, all our writers and everyone who submitted a story. To Babs for creating the perfect cover that they pulled out of nowhere. To the queer horror community for giving me a sense of belonging, and for the friendships I have fostered. To my partner, who came up with the anthology title, and who I love dearly.

To all our trans siblings, whether you're out or not, this is for you.

Collected here are 13 stories of transformation, acceptance, growth and gore. I hope you enjoy them as much as I do.

Love,
Lor Gislason

WORMSPACE

LC VON HESSEN

NO REPUTABLE FETISH club would tell him how to find the Physician. No dungeon or play party, no email or direct message to an online kink discussion board or a BDSM professional, nowhere he dared to probe or stammer out his request saw him treated as anything but a crude edgelord, an undercover cop, or a pathetic and deeply troubled individual. A tap on the shoulder, a tug of the sleeve: *Stop asking. That's fucking stupid. / You need to leave. Don't come here again. / Don't bother us any more. / You're banned. / You're blocked. / Fuck off, man.* Meanwhile, within him, the Worm continued, as always, to turn.

The Physician's forte was neither safe nor sane and only nominally consensual. Many thought she didn't exist and was only an urban legend or a sophomoric in-joke. A living caricature of a mad science domme, it was said that her unhinged clients eagerly volunteered for her clandestine backroom experiments. It was also said that these clients were not seen again. Except, on occasion, as specimens of grotesquerie for well-heeled connoisseurs of Such Things. Most likely, this was mere egotistical self-aggrandizement that had ballooned over time to the level of myth: one could only roll one's eyes at that pretentious scene name alone. *What's your doctorate in, Physician? Is it butt stuff? More like the Proctologist, amirite?*

And yet. His obsession was so intense that he spent nearly all of his not-insubstantial disposable income purchasing information about the Physician and her whereabouts, dropping hefty payments to such upstanding Dark Web users as xVictimizedx and woundfucker88. Naturally he was scammed. A lot. This was less due to naïveté on his part than a resigned belief that such pratfalls were intrinsic to the journey, a test of his sincerity. Such was Jimmy Barton's desperation.

At long last an inquiry had finally, hopefully, borne fruit. Jimmy was instructed to retrieve a sealed missive at a covert drop-off point in a public park in his neighborhood, where it had been deposited by some dubious individual who served as one of her many minions. The Physician's official seal, embossing a glob of black wax, depicted a modified Rod of Asclepius: a skull-headed snake wrapped around a scalpel. The missive contained only an address. Jimmy would have to travel there on his own dime. She would not discuss further matters remotely.

The Physician's alleged address was in the basement level of an otherwise disused warehouse at the outskirts of a moderate-sized American city. Jimmy had to force open the rust-garnished fire door with his shoulder, leaving a smattering of reddish-brown residue on his formal suit jacket. He stepped forward and down, into a tunnel. A long string of sickly fluorescents mounted alongside bulbous metal tubes and ducts in the open ceiling illuminated the nondescript beige-and-white cinder blocks surrounding him.

This was clearly not a commercial dungeon. No wall of whips, crops, ropes, and paddles to show off her repertoire; no boudoir curtains or Inquisitional implements or dramatic lighting to set the mood. Rather than some generically exotic incense to mask patrons' sweat and body odor, it smelled of cold, unsexy damp clinging to the insulation and the cement floor, along with a faint undercurrent of mold.

Aside from the electric hum overhead and Jimmy's tentative steps, the only sound, which steadily increased in volume the further he walked, was a repetitive one-two echoing tap muffled nearby. This one-two rhythm continued for several seconds, then paused briefly, then began again. Some sort of janky machine, he assumed, running within the bowels of the basement.

Jimmy turned the corner.

The Physician held court over this fiefdom of sickly-lit cinder blocks and concrete in a squeaking latex lab coat. A small, plump woman of about 50 or 60 with dark-dyed hair and an elegant mien, she reclined in a black leather office chair, her sensible heels resting on the metal reception desk before her. She idly clicked and unclicked a ballpoint pen while studying the newly-arrived applicant with an utterly inscrutable expression.

Jimmy handed her the missive with its official seal, which she glanced at through cat-eye reading glasses on a silver chain.

"If you've got some kind of snuff fantasy," she began, "you're barking up the wrong tree. I do not kill people." She crossed her legs. "It's not an ethical thing. It's just boring, to me." The Physician spoke with an assured, velvet-lined voice. Her thin lips were painted a deep red verging on black, the color of menstrual clots.

"No, I, I don't . . . " He shook his head, "My name's Jimmy, by the w—"

"I don't care." She waved it off, eyes casing him up and down with distaste. "You still go by 'Jimmy' and you're *how* old?"

Twenty-nine. I'll be 30 next summer, he almost said, before realizing this was a rhetorical question meant to humiliate him.

"Sit."

The lone available chair was a battered beige metal contraption parked in front of the desk. Lowering himself into this chair provoked immediate discomfort from the seat, sagging with a creak of complaint under his ass and thighs; the legs, just short enough to force his knees into acute angles; and the back, which dug into his lower spine at its bottom edge. It was difficult to sit up straight and downright impossible to sit still. He made no objection, certain this was by design.

—Squirm, wormy, squirm—

"Right. Let's get down to it." The Physician swung her legs below the desk, sat up, and tented her fingers. "Why are you here, Jimbo?"

Jimmy Barton clasped his own hands together, hunched forward in the terrible chair, his hair fallen loose, more supplicant than applicant. With little hesitation, he spat it out.

"I want to be flaccid. *All the time.*" The ragged desperation in his voice verged on aggressive.

A smirk of derision as the Physician's eyes flicked down to his crotch.

"Mm. And you can't wait for age to catch up with you."

"No. It has to be as—as soon as possible." He shifted and fidgeted as the Physician briskly shuffled through some mental database.

"Have you tried a regimen of SSRIs? A regular use of narcotics? Alcohol, cocaine?"

"But that's . . . No, no. The effects are just temporary."

"So you'd rather stay sober and possibly dysthymic. Why not a hypno*tissst*?" She teased out the last word with a grin, both of them knowing this suggestion was bullshit. He lowered his head and squeezed his hands together tightly.

"You know, of course, it would have been far cheaper to purchase a male chastity device. A decent cock cage would only cost a fraction, a *tiny* fraction of what you've already spent. Perhaps you could simply throw out the key." She twirled the ballpoint pen between her middle and index fingers. "Anecdotally, it's said to permanently decrease one's ability to develop an erection when worn over an extended period."

"I can't . . . can't wait that long," he mumbled.

"So your impatience is now my problem. Why?"

Jimmy's short nails dug into his dress pants at the knee, too flustered to speak.

"Do you want to be castrated, Jim-Jim?"

"I . . ."

"Because I'll deflate that particular dream right now. Orchiectomy—that's the technical term for human testicle removal—only eliminates the production of sperm, and frequently lowers libido as well, which I'll assume, in your case, is a desirable effect regardless. But—and I'm speaking from personal experience here—it would not fully prevent erection. A common misperception, I know.

"I *could* simply cut your penis off at the root. Testicles, too. All of it." She made a sweeping motion with one loose fist, the ballpoint pen as proxy for a scalpel or straight razor. "Just a Ken doll's groin down there. With a little canal for the urethra. Would that *satisfy* you?"

The sheer contempt in the Physician's voice dripped like bile. "Of course there could very likely be complications, but I genuinely don't care what happens to you." She shrugged. "Any halfway-decent pro-domme could tell you that, but in my case it's true. No reason not to be honest. Since you've made your way here, gone to all that trouble. We ought to be *scrupulously* honest with one another." She fixed him with a hard stare and clutched the pen in both fists. "I know and you know, Jimothy, that you, with your money, could easily find a surgeon to carve up your penile ligaments. What do you *really* want from me?"

Jimmy flushed, sweating, anxiety coursing through his cramped posture. Of course she was on to him. Of course he was lying to himself. She was a professional. She was *the* professional. He could never, ever hide. Crumpled into himself, he considered his words with great care before pushing them out, one by one, as if psychologically constipated. He had never revealed this aloud before and spoke with intense deliberation.

"I want . . . to become . . . a worm."

The Physician did not laugh or scoff, but nodded soberly for him to continue.

It had begun with the nightmare. This dream had followed him as long as he could remember, ever since his tiny mind first had the capacity to visualize objects and record memories: the Worm being birthed, the primordial scream, surrounded on all sides by dirt clotting his throat and intestines, a mouth and anus open forever.

Throughout his childhood with its many outward comforts, the nightfall of his unconscious brought him back to that perfectly cylindrical dirt tunnel with a waiting black eclipse at the end. There was no light of any kind, but in his mind's eye, he saw because he did not need to see: in the tunnel, one had no use for eyes. The tunnel was made for him, by him; he had come to understand that it represented the inmost nature of his soul. If "Jimmy Barton," the name arbitrarily affixed to this lamentable body, were to be bisected vertically from stem to stern, spiritually if not literally, the tunnel is what one would find. In this, the essence of the humble earthworm.

Trapped in a suffocating cocoon that leaked and rotted about him, so ill-fitting around his screaming bones, so tight and constrictive: his soul, he often felt, was caught in the gullet of a great python in the shape of a human man. Joints! Teeth! Hair! The vagaries of smell and taste! The virus of language! The purgatory of custom and culture! Why, *why* was he cursed to be human?

Thus he knew, ultimately, that the scripted, negotiated roles of S/M were not enough, would never be enough. He didn't want to go back to the office, back to his condo, back to his latest round of quotidian errands or distractions, after the scene was over. He didn't want to negotiate a 24/7 role to play. He didn't want to wear a costume, adopt a persona. He wanted, quite simply, to *be*. The primeval ancestor of countless millennia, squirming from water to land, squirming back to negate his own existence. He wanted to enter subspace and never leave, in the manner of one who ingests constant hallucinogens to replicate a state of permanent psychosis until it is no longer a replication. He didn't want to know, or remember, that this was a simulacrum. He wanted to exist without desire and without doubt. To slither and writhe, to eat and excrete, without the human infant's cries and developmental milestones and need for an adult caretaker. To say, to think, *I am a worm now*, but without words or images. To be mindless. To be.

Jimmy explained this as best he could, never having been a very eloquent man. The Physician nodded thoughtfully, listening with care. Then stood, and beckoned him forward.

"Follow me."

She turned the corner and, retrieving a key from a pocket of the latex lab coat, unlocked a nondescript metal door.

The two of them stepped into a long, dim, rectangular room. At the flip of a switch, a row of floodlights blinked on overhead. Revealing, in one strike, both the source of the muffled machine-like rhythm Jimmy had overheard in the tunnel and a prime example of the Physician's skills.

The first thing he noticed was a shapely pair of women's bare legs, outfitted with black patent-leather pumps. These shoes were the source of the rhythm, producing a tinny trip-trap clip-clap sound as they ran across the bare concrete floor: a dull flash of silver as the shoes lifted from the ground exposed a metal plate installed beneath each sole, makeshift tap heels to shift the reverb. The owner of the legs would run one way, come to a halt a few feet before the end of the room, turn sharply on one heel, and run in the other direction; then turn again, repeat the process, back and forth, *ad infinitum*.

From head to low hip, just concealing the crotch and buttocks, the figure's body was entirely bound up in multiple layers of latex. The topmost layer, shrink-wrapped around a torso with arms crossed mummy-like over the chest, was a striking iridescent grey-blue, embellished with scale print. It—she?—resembled a grand bipedal chrysalis, or would have if not for the absurd presence of a goggle-eyed, gawp-mouthed fish head atop the shoulders, alongside flopping latex fins and cosmetic gills.

"She was the scion of a good family," said the Physician at Jimmy's side. "'Good' simply meaning ridiculously wealthy. You would certainly have heard of them, unless you'd grown up Amish or in some sort of survivalist commune. A party girl, socialite. A very chipper girl. Early twenties, or so she was back then. A Disney princess type." The Physician mimed a brief curtsey. "She came to me wanting to become a mermaid. She was *quite* adamant about that. Although, to be frank, she wasn't at all specific."

Jimmy stared at the running figure, with its flapping false fins and mouth, its pin-up girl gams, and understood.

"Look at her run," said the Physician, with uncommon warmth. "She's swimming."

Tip-tap-tip-tap-tip-tap-tip-tap—squeeeak—Tip-tap-tip-tap-tip-tap-tip-tap

"She's fed with a concealed IV tube. Urinates and defecates on a timer: there's a metal bucket set aside for that purpose. Her body has been completely depilated because fish, of course, do not have fur outside of novelty taxidermist gaffs." She pointed to the mermaid's false head. "They're well-hidden, but she has two small holes for her nostrils in deference to her mammalian need for oxygen. Eventually I think she ought to have a blowhole installed. Her arms are quite withered by now, little Tyrannosaur winglets. They're due for amputation soon. She can hear, a little. She knows simple commands."

The Physician sharply clapped her hands twice in succession. "*¡Olé!*"

The mermaid paused in mid-stride. She stood at the end of the room, one leg stiff and bracing, the other stomping at the ground and kicking back imaginary dirt before angling her torso like a primed cannon and barreling forward in a sprint to charge at an invisible red cape. Another two claps from the Physician and she paused again before continuing to "swim" at her normal pace.

"Is she lobotomized?" Jimmy whispered.

"Oh no." The Physician smiled. "She's a mermaid."

Jimmy's eyes were fixed on the mermaid's legs. Her calves were lithe, yet quite muscular. A thin, glistening trail trickled down from her inner thighs to trace the path of her route on the concrete, and he wondered if it was merely sweat from the combination of tight latex and her unceasing exertions, or if it also indicated a curious, constant arousal.

Determining he had seen enough, the Physician stepped back out of the room as Jimmy followed. She locked the door behind them, leaving the mermaid to run in darkness.

"Now think, and think hard, Jimbles, before you give your answer." She fanned a hand at the door, nodding soberly, then stared back into him. "Knowing what you know now, would you still like to request my services?"

And Jimmy Barton looked down, from the Physician's keen eyes and firm lips to his own fidgeting fingers, to his scuffed businessman's brogues, to the cold concrete beneath; and he shrank, bit by bit, bone by bone, into nothing, the Worm turning through his nerves, his innards, the pathetic folds of his cerebrum. The tunnel opened at last, and he could only fall through to the black eclipse.

Some time later, a new applicant has dedicated large sums of money to locating the Physician, and their investment has recently paid off. In the maintenance level of a disused office complex, with tentative steps past bare sheetrock walls, they clutch a black-sealed missive in one sweating hand, nose full of the lingering smell of stale sawdust from never-finished construction.

A slow, regimented back-and-forth clomp echoes from an unseen room as the Physician flips a light switch to show off an example of her previous work. There, in a man-sized plexiglass trough full of dirt: a near-blind, toothless spine, arms amputated and legs severed and truncated into a tail, wrapped in a glistening non-skin of ringed pink latex. It flails and squirms, mouthfuls of dirt passing through the callused gums of its perpetually open maw, back out through its cloaca. And if the applicant cares to look closely enough, in the lone visible eye lurks a horrid but unmistakable spark of intelligence.

THE HAUNTING OF AIDEN FINCH

THEO HENDRIE

THE LOST HIKER saw the phone before he saw the body. The tinted red of his flashlight shone against it, nestled among the leaves. Yet, in the dim light he almost stumbled over the soft *thing* beside it. They were lying side by side, person and object, both of them bloody and face-down on the forest floor.

He had imagined coming across a scene like this many times. Perhaps he had a morbid mind, or perhaps spending so much time alone in the depths of the National Parks simply had that kind of effect. In his imagination, he would have rushed over, checked the body for a pulse, been the hero. In reality, one look at the body by his feet told him that it was too late for heroics. The way it was lying was *wrong*—at once too stiff and too soft, as if it had contracted and then expanded, almost spilling over its own edges. The head caved in on itself like squashed food. Fragments of bone and brain and hair flecked the ground around it, reminding him of paint flicked carelessly from the end of a brush. From the clothes and the back of the bloody head, the hiker guessed the kid to be male, an older teen. But he didn't want to look too closely.

So instead he picked up the phone. Turning it over, he could see the edges of the crack spider-webbing across the screen. They spread out from the top right corner like the lace edges of the doilies in his grandmother's house. The faint traces of bloody fingerprints still showed on the screen, gleaming in the beam of the flashlight. For a second he worried that he had ruined some key evidence but even he could see that they were too smeared and mangled to be of any use in an investigation.

When the screen flickered on, he felt an undefined relief to find there was no password protecting it.

It only got weirder when he swiped up to get to the homescreen. There were no apps and none of the social media he might have expected for a kid of this age. There was only the default browser and other pre-installed crap. It was as if someone had wiped the phone clean of all data and then placed it back where they found it. Placed it waiting to be found.

The hiker tapped half-heartedly on the camera roll. To his surprise, it loaded up, full of videos and photos. Unable to resist the thought that he might soon learn the dead boy's name, he scrolled through. It seemed right somehow to start at the beginning and so he clicked on the oldest video.

VIDEO ONE

A blurred thumb covered most of the screen before pulling away to reveal the interior of some shitheap car and a lanky teen leaning back in his seat, framed horizontally. The phone wobbled on the dashboard, almost fell and was caught by that same blurred hand. When it was steady again, the teen smiled. "Well . . . I never thought I'd be making one of these but . . . here we are."

He was skinny with a mop of sandy blonde hair and dark eyes that betrayed a mischievous glint even on the small screen. He had a round, almost feminine face and his voice was high. It made him look young. On his jacket were a smattering of button badges. One of them said 'He/him' with a trans pride flag behind it.

"Hi, my name is Aiden Finch," he continued, "and this is my voice . . . about twenty minutes on T."

The hiker smiled, thinly. Already the body had a name. This was good.

"Oh Christ, I'm already cringing at myself." Aiden laughed, on-screen. Though his words were self-deprecating, the laugh was free, his face open and joyous. "I really never thought I'd be one of those trans guys that makes transition updates on YouTube. But I can't believe I'm finally on testosterone. I've waited so long for this, and . . . I don't care if it's cringey. I can't wait to share this journey with you all."

The video paused on a frame of Aiden's hand reaching for the phone.

The hiker hesitated. It didn't seem likely that he would find out much more than a name and it was time to go find help. But he wasn't ready to stop snooping yet. He scrolled to the next video.

VIDEO TWO

The phone was on the floor, its low angle showing Aiden sitting on a tartan picnic blanket in the middle of some grassy park. "Hi, my name is Aiden Finch, and this is my voice one month on T."

He paused for a second, fiddling with a piece of grass. He ripped the stalk out of the ground. "I don't think much has changed yet . . . at least not anything I can show you—if you know, you know. I'm trying to enjoy the journey but I'm so impatient."

The hiker found himself distracted while Aiden kept chatting away to the camera. There was a slight blur on the lens, small enough to seem like it was floating in the background. If he looked at it just long enough, in just the right way, the shadow began to look like the outline of a disjointed figure enveloped in a veil.

VIDEO THREE

They were back in Aiden's car again, on the edge of a parking lot. There was a sliver of a view through the passenger window showing a thin grass verge, then a cracked sidewalk, then the busy street beyond. Cars whirred up and down the street while Aiden spoke. There was a raspiness to his voice now, as if he had a slight cough. "Hi, my name is Aiden Finch, and this is my voice two months on T."

In the background, someone dressed as a ghost walked down the street. It was the classic Halloween look with a white sheet draped over their head. From this distance, he couldn't see the face. They carried a black balloon, which bobbed over their head as if eager to break free.

VIDEO FOUR

The car again. This time, Aiden had been through a drive-through, if the Taco Bell wrappers strewn across the passenger seat were anything to go by. "Hi," he said, grinning at the camera around a mouthful of food. He paused and swallowed. "Sorry, let me try that again. Hi, my name is Aiden Finch, and this is my voice three months on T."

Distant movement caught the hiker's eye. There, in the background of the shot, another sheet ghost with the same black balloon. The hiker stared at it for a moment, a question beginning to form.

He closed out of the video and looked at the details for the file—this had happened in May, nowhere near Halloween. A kid going to a costume party perhaps? But two kids, exactly a month apart, wearing the exact same costume and both just happening to stumble across the same kid in his car filming himself?

The hiker shook his head as if trying to clear cobwebs from between his ears. It was bizarre to be sure, but there went that morbid mind of his again. It was just a coincidence.

He swept his flashlight in a circle. He had fixed the red cellophane over the bulb months ago. It helped preserve his night vision. But now he found himself wishing that he hadn't, wishing that the beam would stretch a little further into the suffocating darkness of the trees.

VIDEO FIVE

There was a sheet ghost again in the next video—could it be the same one? It was closer this time. It stood a little behind and to the left of the car, visible in the frame from the moment the video began. Aiden had spotted it too. That much was obvious from the way his eyes kept flitting up to the rear-view mirror, checking if his spectral audience was still present.

"Hey guys, check this out," he said, reaching forward to pick the camera up. The video wobbled for a second and then settled. Now it was facing the ghost directly through the rear window of the car.

The hiker frowned. It was still too far away to pick out many details, but something about the way the thing held itself so still unsettled him. The eyes, just two holes in a blank face, reminded him of an arachnid, alien and unknowing. It brought a rarely used word to his mind: pareidolia—the way that people interpret shapes in inanimate objects to be faces. Try as he might, he couldn't imagine a real face hiding behind those roughly cut holes. Though it stood like a person, everything in him screamed that it was *other*.

"I keep seeing these everywhere," Aiden said. "Like, literally everywhere I go. I thought it must be some kind of movie promotion or something, but I can't find anybody talking about it. LA is crazy, man."

VIDEO SIX

Aiden was his usual cheerful self when the video first started. "Hi, my name is Aiden Finch, and this is my voice five month on T. You can totally hear a huge difference now! But I'm getting voice cracks like a teenager . . ."

A shadow fell across the screen. The sheet ghost was back, now looming so close that it obscured the sunlight falling through the car window.

The smile dropped from the kid's mouth so fast it was like he'd been punched. He froze for a moment and then, a new expression twisted his face. "Leave me the fuck alone!" Aiden's voice sounded tinny on the phone speaker but clearly strained. "Do you hear me? I said leave me alone!"

The thing that looked like a ghost only stared, looking blankly from the two holes cut in its plain white face.

IMAGE ONE

A screenshot of a dark website with small cramped text filled the screen. A banner with a font like dripping blood proclaimed this to be the 'Cryptid Warehouse.'

THE THING WITH THE BLACK BALLOON:

An unknown creature in the California area which disguises itself as a childish sheet ghost. According to local legend, it feeds on fear. However, the creature is unable to sense or identify the phobias of its prey. Instead, it chooses a form it believes humans find universally terrifying—since it is a costume that we choose on All Hallows' Eve over and over again. The creature is rumoured to live deep in the woods. No one knows the significance of the balloon, only that it always carries one while stalking its victims.

Beneath that was a rough sketch, showing something vaguely akin to a sheet ghost but taller. It had legs as long and thin and dark as a spider's. In one clawed hand it clutched a string with an awfully familiar black balloon.

IMAGE TWO

This time the screenshot included a blurred black and white photograph of the woods. Someone had helpfully circled a smudge between the trees. If he squinted at it, it looked almost like a ghost with something dark and orb-like hovering above it. The caption beneath the image read:

The Black Balloon Ghost—this forest spirit stalks its victims. It can only be stopped if you find its lair deep within the woods and destroy the heart it keeps there.

VIDEO SEVEN

The video was shaking so badly that it took the hiker a moment to figure out what he was looking at. When the view finally focused, he realised it was poking through a curtain, looking out the window from a low angle so that part of the sill obscured the view. It shifted slightly, showing a darkened backyard. A bike lay abandoned on the lawn. Crazy paving led the way from the front door to the gate. And there, at the gate, stood the ghost, waiting on its spindly legs.

The camera moved again, the view blurring with the speed and then refocusing to show Aiden, slumped against the wall beside the window, out of sight. He held the phone out in front of him in one shaking hand. It was dark in the room, but the soft glow of the screen glinted on the tear tracks on his cheeks.

"I don't know what to do," he whispered. "The police won't come anymore. I called them three times last week, but they couldn't find anything. They think I'm prank calling or something. No one will listen to me anymore. And it won't go away."

The video juddered to a halt. The hiker looked away and found himself staring at something worse. The body that had once belonged to Aiden Finch lay where it had fallen, seeming to glare at the hiker accusingly even with its face turned away. He kept finding his eyes drawn to it. This wasn't morbid curiosity—he needed the reminder that this wasn't just some stupid prank or the kid's media project. The stranger things became on the videos the more he felt that he was only dreaming. But somehow, Aiden had died. And the only files left on this phone all seemed to point in one impossible direction.

PENULTIMATE VIDEO

They were back in the car but from a new perspective this time. Aiden's shaky breathing rattled in the background as he held the phone out to the window. The near shapeless form of the sheet ghost reared right behind the glass.

The camera lingered on the creature just long enough for the image to burn into the hiker's mind. Even now it looked almost like some kid dressing up for Halloween in his bed linens. But there was that *wrongness* again. The limbs beneath the sheet were too long, too thin to belong to any person, let alone a child. What little skin peeped through the holes in the sheet looked grey, cracked and undeniably dead. When it opened its mouth, it revealed a row of sharp, grinding teeth, and behind them the warm pink of its tongue, utterly alive and hungry.

Afterwards, the hiker wouldn't be able to explain what it was that made him think *hungry*. It was just a mouth, just a tongue. But looking into it, he had known with as much certainty as he had ever known anything, it would swallow him whole if it could only reach him.

Somehow it occurred to him anew: he was alone in the woods with a fresh body, and that whatever had caused this probably hadn't gone all that far. The last cool tendrils of shock drifted from him as adrenaline shot through his veins. He had never felt unsafe in the woods before, no matter how lost he became or what nighttime rustlings he heard. He lived with the trees on his back doorstep his whole life, after all, and the wild was like a second home to him. Now though, he found himself wishing he hadn't strayed so far from the beaten path.

He hesitated before scrolling to the next video. But there was nothing to do but keep watching. He was only here to bear witness. He wanted to know how it ended.

FINAL VIDEO

As the video loaded, the hiker realised with a chill that the images on screen showed the same woods that he now stood in. Only in the video, it was daytime. A small amount of sunlight, tinged green by the thick canopy of leaves above, filtered through to illuminate the way. Aiden was out of frame, phone out in front of him to film his progress. He was speaking softly.

The hiker pressed the volume button on the side of the phone, once, twice, three times. He held the phone closer to his face, straining to hear.

"I'm going to end this," Aiden whispered. "I know it's insane. But this thing . . . whatever it is, it's real. And I'm going to stop it. I . . . I have to show you. I have to film this so you'll know what's happening to me is real."

For a while, the video continued in much the same way, shaky and uncertain. Then in response to something the camera hadn't picked up, Aiden whirled around. There, a few paces behind him, was the sheet ghost. It walked, taking big juddering footsteps, like the scuttle of a centipede. Though its upper body was deathly still, it moved quickly.

Aiden didn't wait to see what would happen when it caught up to him. He took off running, the phone falling to his side. The view bounced around jarringly showing the leaves on the forest floor disappearing beneath his rapid feet. The hiker found that he was holding his breath and forced himself to exhale. What use was rooting for this kid on the screen when the ending waited dead and cold by his feet?

Aiden's breath came in short, sharp bursts. The phone swung up as he twisted around to see if it was still behind him. Nothing. The forest was still and quiet. He turned back around, still holding the phone out as if it could ward off whatever would happen next.

The ghost stepped out from behind a tree, close enough to fill the whole screen. Aiden screamed and, at the same time, the thing opened its mouth. And kept opening it, wider and wider, stretching further than it should like a snake unhinging its jaw. Its teeth were long and serrated, its tongue twitching and eager. The camera pointed straight up into that gaping maw, shaking slightly but never moving away. The hiker was transfixed, unable to tear his eyes away from the glow of the screen.

The phone dropped to the floor. For a second all that was visible were the branches of the trees far above. And then moving into frame, the sheet ghost, its stretched mouth clinging to Aiden's head. Its body shivered as Aiden oozed a little further down its throat, sliding in up to his neck. His body twitched and shuddered, feet beating against the ground. There was a soft, wet sound. It was the same kind of squelch the ground made when you pulled your foot loose from the mud after a storm. The creature's bulging mouth shrank a little as Aiden's skull gave. And then the blood came, bright and red and hot, running down from between the thing's terrible gnawing teeth. Even now its mouth kept moving, open, closed, shoving the needle-sharp teeth into tattered flesh. Again. Again. Each bite a hook to draw the body a little deeper in.

As suddenly as it had grabbed him, the ghost opened its mouth. The body landed with a thump out of frame and the screen went dark.

The hiker lowered the phone, unable or perhaps unwilling to process the things he had seen. He spared one last glance at Aiden, pocketed the phone for evidence, and turned away.

As he did so, the reddish glow of his flashlight hit the trees ahead of him. But instead of the pockets of black between the trunks that he was used to, his eyes snagged on something up ahead. In the distance, just within the reach of the light, a sheet ghost stood still and watched him, its black balloon held aloft.

COMING OUT

DEREK DES ANGES

LP30958 IS ONE of those prisons that's described as "notorious" without anyone troubling to go into specifics about what it's notorious *for*. It's best that we leave it that way: the imagination can fill in all of the unfortunate gaps quite easily.

Bren McCool's reasons for being sentenced to LP30958 are also best left in the past, along with his crimes: their relevance is only that they landed him here in LP30958, on the wrong side of the filtration doors, on the wrong side of the law, and with unsettling rapidity one bad afternoon two years into his sentence, on the wrong side of El Carnicero.

This is very bad news for Bren McCool, because although Bren has been careful to retain an aura of impenetrable masculine violence and a physique which should deter all but the most heavily armoured of cops, he has not successfully cultivated the networks of influence necessary in a closed system like LP30958, or indeed any institution. Arguably, that's what got him here, too, but as we've said: that's not relevant to this story.

El Carnicero is very good at making friends and he is also very good at making unwanted orifices in his enemies, a skillset from which he derives his nickname. He was originally serving time for the minor misdemeanour of animal cruelty: the cruelty was to the Mayor's dogs, which increased the sentence far beyond those of mere rapists and murderers. Each time he falls out with one of his new pals, his sentence increases. It is possible he may end up spending his life in prison for kicking a dog in the balls.

Prison being prison, it doesn't matter what you're in for at first. Once you're in, the mutant social pressures of the incarcerated produce violent seasons and a weather system all of their own, a hundred different reasons and a hundred different victims, all with one solution: someone shanks someone else to come out on top of the shit-heap for a day.

Bren McCool is taking a dump when things go from "bad, to "worse", to "even fucking worse".

One thing that has never changed about prison since the concept of carcerality was invented is that it's absolutely impossible to shit in peace. Under a clouded and toxic sky, in a world rife with surveillance equipment and a truly mind-boggling amount of ways to consume porn, this remains a constant. In prison, there is nowhere private to unload.

He is testing this theory on the toilet in an otherwise empty cell which is normally shared with three other men (or perhaps, like him, they are only men-on-paper, he's never asked), not really wondering why exactly the cell *is* deserted in the middle of the day when the answer to the unasked question arrives in the form of El Carnicero and his two friends, who are both very large, very nasty, and very armed with very homemade blades.

Bren McCool accepts that today is not going to improve.

There is a short discussion in the vein of a negotiation.

El Carnicero agrees that Bren McCool's infraction is *probably* not intentional. He then makes it amiably clear he has no desire to put any terminating punctuation in the sentence of Bren McCool's life. He instead offers him the disciplinary ordeal that functions more, perhaps, as a semi-colon. With the emphasis on the colon.

While Bren McCool is not entirely happy with this outcome, he is significantly relieved that he's not about to exit the world of the living. There are, he believes, a number of people in the world of the dead who aren't wild about the prospect of having to see him again and he's sure they have a hand in keeping him firmly on the opposite side of this one-way door.

He's also in no position to argue: there is a prison jumpsuit around his ankles, plastic shoes on his feet and he's currently sitting on a very uncomfortable ring of unbreakable metal above a cone of cold water that he at least had the presence of mind to flush when he saw El Carnicero. There's nothing he can use to defend himself, barring the apology he's already made.

Some things are timeless. Outside technology marches the population ever-closer to sinking, but in here, the future stalled in the previous two centuries.

They pull him from the toilet. For a moment he considers clinging like a barnacle to the can but he knows from first-hand accounts and the accompanying evidence of his own eyes that they will just cut off his fingers if he tries. Bren McCool would like to retain the use of his fingers: he's always had a certain fondness for being able to flip the bird, or, say, eat, and dial telephones.

Perhaps it is better to draw a veil of discretion over the precise moment of injury. It will come back to haunt Bren McCool later, when he is sweating and straining and bleeding before the morphine kicks in. It will do us no good to witness it.

It is not quick, but it is, in its way, less terrible than it could have been. Because the punctures are on the *inside* of his colon alone and do not break the skin of his belly, he will reduce his risk of a staph infection. Because El Carnicero is a man of his word, it is only once: the multiple punctures are simply a function of how a man's colon twists and turns. Because Bren McCool is, despite the standard of prison food, a relatively healthy individual, he will not die from shock. Because the world has come a long way in terms of medicine, even if it hasn't caught up in terms of kindness.

All the same, Bren McCool is not having a very good day when the warden finds him, sighs, and goes to call the medical team.

⚧

In the prison infirmary, Bren McCool listens in a red-tinged haze of artificial wellbeing to phrases that make very little sense, and ones which unfortunately do, such as "colostomy bag".

He tries to object to this. He tries to explain walking around with a bag of shit taped to himself in a general prison population is effectively a death sentence. He attempts to summon everything he knows about hygiene, which is granted not a lot, to offer up the reality of his impending death from recurrent infections and likely end in a lake of his own diverted shit.

However, he is full of hospital-grade narcotics, with the doctor's first language being "tired and fed up with treating the injuries of idiot prisoners", and the doctor's second language is not one he speaks, so what comes out of Bren McCool's mouth is: "I will die of poop."

The doctor sighs at him and turns to her male subordinate. Bren McCool thinks that he, the subordinate, may be a nurse, rather than another doctor. She, the doctor, says something he doesn't understand. The nurse shrugs. He won't die; it's increasingly hard to do that, even in this age of new diseases.

Bren McCool sleeps.

Three days later he is transferred to a solitary cell with a lone copy of a religious text for a religion he doesn't follow, and a narrow sliver of light from twenty-five percent of a window which slithers like a raindrop down the opposite wall over the course of a day. His few effects from his old cell are not given to him. He has a new jumpsuit: this one is larger, to make room for the bag of shit.

"Two bags of shit," says the warden cheerfully, when he notes this. "You, and it."

"Thanks," says Bren McCool .

He is still taking slow-release painkillers—not enough over the course of a day to achieve what he'd like—and a semi-liquid diet while his brain slowly liquifies from boredom when he spots something in his cell which oughtn't be in his cell.

It is not the drip from the ceiling: this is as much a part of prison architecture as the steel toilet bowls, riveted-on basins, and cold concrete floors. It is not the grim array of notches in the institutional grey paint counting the days, weeks, months; nor the inevitable far-right symbols scratched into the steel of the toilet bowl that he only ever pisses in. Those are to prisons what leaves are to trees.

Bren McCool is walking clockwise around his cell like an imprisoned bear, thinking about his body, how it is no longer his body but *medicine's* body, how this doesn't feel any different to it being *work's* body and how sometimes he wonders if it would be any worse to cut off his balls, since they keep sticking to his legs and no one is going to fuck him with a bag of shit hanging out of his stomach. He is thinking about how he plans to make sure the wardens get the task of changing the bag of shit every single day until his parole, because the only thing he can ever do to get back at them for being so pathetically useless and so senselessly, boringly cruel is to make them touch his still-warm, never-shat turds in a neat package—because he no longer cares if the whole thing just backs up and kills him—but it'll look bad for their record if it does.

He is still walking clockwise around his cell when he

spots three beautiful sun-yellow discs a little to the left of the drip from the ceiling, below the outflow pipe from the toilet, which has been buttressed and repaired so many times it still eats red rust out of its own brackets. There are three golden discs, and when he gets down on his hands and knees, he can see their long thin umbrella-handles.

They are little mushrooms.

Bren McCool stares at the little yellow mushrooms and the little yellow trio stare back at him with pupil-less eyes.

Well, he thinks, *you're not meant to be here.*

He wonders what they eat. What there can possibly be, in this dark little room which is driving him mad, along with the echoing sound of his own thoughts, the distant clangs of prison life and the fact that he's got a fucking hole in his abdomen for an indeterminate period of time—possibly the rest of his life—and that he's got a bag of faecal matter taped to him at all times.

What do mushrooms eat?

Shit, probably.

It turns out there's one benefit to being a freak, a disfigured lumbering shape, a known recipient of a prison shank in an orifice not intended for insertion of anything but the most carefully-shaped of phallic objects.

To comply with the kind of laws newspapers sneer at, there must be "educational and redemptive opportunities" provided to prisoners. This is lip-service to human progress. It is the twenty-second century, and prisons are an embarrassment to the liberal half of the press.

To ensure no one actually murders anyone in front of the external educators there is a division of 'classes'. All those who are likely to die from being shoved too hard—the elderly, guys who came to prison on purpose because they don't have a pension, the ones who need cancer treatment, who attempted suicide and didn't *quite* die—are lumped together in what's loosely referred to elsewhere as the *Losers' Wing*.

As an inmate of the Losers' Wing, Bren McCool finally has access to a lathe.

What he does *not* have access to is that which no longer has access to *him*. Which means the traditional use of the lathe, of turning any bit of scrap anyone can get his hands on into a deadly, or at least incapacitating weapon, is pointless.

Whitty, the group's most recent attempted suicide, is banned from the lathe. His arm is in a sling from the last time he went near it: now he's a fractured machine, in the process of being rebuilt. The lathe, on the other hand, is fine. Bren McCool has already claimed his spot and doesn't know what the hell to do with it.

Machine shop's teacher, Andy, is a long thin white man with long thin hair that is thinner on the top. He is pleasant to everyone equally, divulging little of his life outside his visits beyond that he once worked in an auto garage. A thin white scar crawls up the inside of his left arm that branches and splits like an aerial photograph of a river delta. It looks as if a white worm is spreading beneath his flesh.

Sometimes, he briefly mentions the news; a man's prosthetic penis, connected to the internet, stopped allowing him to urinate unless he paid the ransom. Andy says, "Unfortunately, they picked someone who was into that. But his insurance doesn't cover a catheter."

Bren McCool's relationship with his own, non-prosthetic penis has not exactly improved since his incident. He still doesn't appreciate the humour, but says nothing.

Andy says, "Don't get tied down to the idea that this has to be useful, McCool. It can be expressive as well. Don't forget people use welding to create sculptures."

Someone mutters the one thing he thinks Bren McCool aches to express, a dirty little word, but when Bren McCool whips around he can't see who said it.

It's not like he can do anything about it in his current condition.

He tries to make the smallest possible metal vase. It comes out looking more like a nitrous oxide capsule, the sort that litter the streets outside every weekend, the ones that crunch and rust underfoot, laughing-gas confetti from the culinary trade.

Bren McCool buffs the open-ended capsule until it shines.

He is thinking idly about the movement of spider legs and a horror film he saw as a teenager where a woman's vagina turned into a spider when it turns out that, while making a shiv is off the cards, one of the dog-ends of the prison has just managed to embarrass himself by creating something *else* verboten on the lathe and is receiving a humiliating dressing-down.

The scolding, mild as it is, comes back into focus because everyone around him is snickering:

The culprit, a red-faced forty-something fruit known only as Big Mary—in reference more to his proclivities than his size—is examining the ceiling.

Andy is holding what resembles the beginnings of a copper pipe dildo in both hands with a look of disappointment.

The rest of the Losers' Wing have begun shooting glances at Bren McCool, who has often thought that people in here suspected him but comforted himself previously with the knowledge they have no idea what it is they suspect him *of*, because he's never been entirely sure either.

"Gareth, if you stick something like this up your ass, you will end up like McCool."

And that is why everyone is looking at Bren McCool. Because they all know, of course, why he has joined them.

Bren McCool furiously buffs the little thin-necked vase, and begins collecting up the fine, straight rods which Andy has been using to demonstrate how to make a ring. He imagines them unfolding like the legs of an insect. He imagines them unfolding inside a wound. Releasing something they've caught.

For obvious reasons, they are not allowed to remove projects from metal shop.

For obvious reasons, 'not allowed' rarely stops anyone.

There is a new guard overseeing his isolation cell. The guard doesn't like being on isolation cell duty any more than Bren McCool likes being in an isolation cell, and he tries to make conversation about it, when the inmate is trying, as best he can, to figure out if he can dump his nutrient drink onto the mushrooms without being caught, and whether this will make them bigger, or kill them. It's not helping *him* very much, after all, and Lord knows he does not need to get any bigger himself.

The guard says, "I don't know what it is with you people. All obsessed with growing things. As soon as you're locked up, half of you turn into gardeners."

Bren McCool thinks, *what else can we do to change the world we're in?*

He says nothing. It's not even true. Men destroy their cells, paint the walls with shit, pin up pictures torn out of magazines with chewed gum, scratch their names into the grey misery scraped over the bare blocks, it's all the same urge: *I am real and I am here. Look what I can do. Look at how I can change the world.*

Taking his silence for a cue to keep talking, or at least knowing he can't do anything to shut him up, the guard raises his already-loud voice; "Now brewing, I get. You guys wanna be high all the time. Shit, I'd wanna be high all the time if I was in a cell. I wanna be high all the time just *looking* at you sorry fucks. What gets me, though? See, my uncle makes wine. Really nasty wine, but you can't say it to his face, of course. But I know where you get the juice. We give you ungrateful assholes the juice, and you go and ferment it. What gets me, where do you get the *yeast*?"

The guard bangs the flat of his hand on the door, frustrated.

"You guys smuggle everything in here, right? Drugs, phones, knives. Porn. Really sick porn sometimes. Who the *fuck* is smuggling yeast?"

Bren McCool shrugs and wills the guard to go away. The bag in his lap is slowly filling up with shit. He knows by now that if he throws it at the door, none of it will reach the guard, he'll just lose his shop privileges, and it will make his cell stink. *He* will be the one to clean it up. *But wouldn't it be nice*, he thinks. *Wouldn't it be nice to shut him up?*.

"It was driving me crazy," the guard confesses, conspiratorial at the little window, four inches back from the side of the door that contains Bren McCool and the tiny vase he's placed under the mushrooms to make them look like flowers. "So I ZipSearched it, right?"

There's another bang on the door, this one of triumph.

"You know what I find? You motherfuckers don't have to smuggle it at all! It's everywhere. It's in the *air*. Everywhere in the wind. You're getting free yeast *out of the air* that comes in through the window!"

Bren McCool leans back on the bed, looks at the narrow slot of a window. *At least we're getting something for free*, he admits.

He dreams, surrounded by the grinding and crunching of gears as somewhere outside his cell, an automated security door malfunctions.

He dreams, drifting in the unease of a place which is never silent and never still, but in which all the disturbance is out of his reach and out of his control.

He dreams of yellow suns, tiny mushrooms growing from the stoma in his abdomen, and their caps have sucking mouths like flies or leeches. They spiral out of the hole in his belly and wrap around his legs. They chew a hole in the bag which hangs from him and hundreds and thousands of gears burst out. The gears fall to the floor. They sprout into more yellow mushrooms.

Bren McCool wakes covered in sweat. His bag has slipped. His belly hurts.

The rumour goes that the security door was hacked by Queer Terrorists. "This," the guard says, "is what they get for connecting everything to the internet." They won't be making *that* mistake twice, so Bren McCool—sweating on his back—can quit thinking he's going to escape.

It takes a month of antibiotics to shift the infection.

This doctor is new. He looks about twelve. He says, conversationally, past Bren McCool's head to the talkative guard, "Penicillin's a mould. It's best not to write things off just because they seem useless." Bren McCool realises there's a longer conversation taking place that he wasn't aware of until now. He tries to listen.

"I read there's yeast in the air," says the guard, who clearly wants everyone to know that he's an educated man, a man of *science*, as the doctor slips the IV for the broad-spectrum antibiotics into Bren McCool's arm without consulting him at all. "You reckon that's why all these idiots keep coming in with crotch rot?"

"No," says the doctor with a smirk, "that's because they don't *wash*."

He slaps Bren McCool on the shoulder. His hand is smooth and soft and if Bren McCool wasn't slumped in the orange plastic chair while he perspires and very slightly bleeds, the doctor wouldn't be able to reach his shoulder at all.

"Try to keep this in place and stay clean, pal," says the doctor. "Or you're going to be back in here and I might not be able to save you the next time. You aren't a machine. You *grow* things if you don't keep dirt out of your insides."

The guard is on his phone, in direct contravention of the rules of the prison, which Bren McCool knows by heart. "Says here," he observes, "Penicillin is a fungus."

"Mould, yeast, it's all fungus," says the doctor dismissively.

Bren McCool's looking at the IV bag. The contents are clear. There's no sign of the little yellow suns inside it but he thinks: *it's full of them. It's full of them and so am I.*

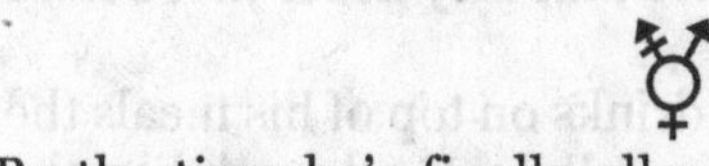

By the time he's finally allowed back in shop the little yellow mushrooms have disappeared. It's only by crawling on his hands and knees like a man worshipping at a mosque that he can see tiny little yellow nubbins erupting further along the wall at floor level.

Bren McCool can't get to the lathe for half the class because the suicide guy's cast is off and he's busy making something he says is a bracelet for his mom. Someone else has the PCB-printer. Bren McCool plays with the rods. He gets the metal drill, instead. Outside the prison they've got machines that walk and talk and shoot perps in the knees and inside it's grandfather tech.

By the end of class, he hasn't been near the lathe once and he's experiencing something like a frenzy; sweat rolls down the back of his neck in tides and the walls of the room contract and expand and he has in his hands a jointed basket whose shape changes with each movement.

Andy called it a kinetic sculpture.

Bren McCool calls it the same size as his bag of shit. Alone in his cell he discovers he's right.

He spends the evening trying to fit it to his body: the dream of mechanical spider legs emerging from his midriff he has afterward is only to be expected, but it still wakes him with a shout of fear, clutching at the stoma as if it's about to expand and swallow the cell, the prison, and him with it, like a black hole.

"You're starving," says the doctor. A third doctor. This one's Black. She has shaved her head down to fine knots. She has cheekbones you could slice cheese on. Bren McCool thinks that before this, he would have fallen in love with her at once.

It's probably better for her that they never met before this.

"He gets the nutritional drinks on top of his meals the last guy said," the guard says sulkily. He doesn't like the doctor; it makes Bren McCool like her more.

She won't last, because she gives a damn.

"He's not getting the benefit of them," she says, showing the guard blood test results that will be as meaningless to Bren McCool as they are to the guard. "It's not just a question of calories in and health out. He's not a machine. There's still a problem with his digestion. I'm going to see if the director will clear some more testing."

"He won't agree to it," says the guard, surreptitiously wiping the sole of his shoe against the table-leg. He's right, of course. The funding isn't for *tests*. It's for stopping the human rights charities from suing the prison for not doing the bare minimum they're required to by law.

"You *are* eating?" the doctor asks Bren McCool directly, at last. "You're not on some kind of hunger strike, are you?"

"Sure," Bren McCool says, thinking of the place where the new crop of golden sun mushrooms is twirling like phoenix feathers out of the grime of his cell floor. "We're eating fine. We're fine."

Before the next fever gets bad enough that anyone notices, he eats the mushrooms.

"We're fine," he tells the ceiling of the cell.

"Shut up, McCool," says the guard.

Neither mushrooms nor machines are male or female, he thinks in a state of high delirium, clinging to the side of his cot like he's being tossed on a stormy sea.

He tries to tell himself he didn't really care about that before he was high as fuck in a prison whose walls are crumbling. He tries to tell himself he didn't think like this before he had to hold his digestive process in his hands. He tries to tell himself that he was doing a great job of being a man.

He can't even remember why that was so important.

When the fever breaks, it is to the persistent sound of dripping from the ceiling. Something in the cell above has broken and sprung a leak. One of the guys probably ripped the sink from the wall again. Maybe to throw at someone. Maybe he just wanted a change of scenery.

Bren McCool burrows through the thick earthen blanket of consciousness and makes some alterations to the so-called kinetic sculpture, the thing he's privately dubbed the *shit basket*. The supposed vase that resembles a nitrous capsule. To the stoma. To the nature of his body. To the barriers between himself and the place he is in.

The guard opens the small window and says, "What the hell are you doing in there, McCool? Get this stuff off the window or you're going to be in shit deeper than your damn asshole scars."

Bren McCool says, "We're coming out in a minute, please get back."

"What's that?"

"We're coming out."

The guard scowls into the mass of white strands, like fluffy cobwebs that cover most of the hole where the food window opens. They seem to be creeping closer. "I don't care about your gay shit, McCool, get this stuff of the window."

"Not like that," they reply, amused.

"Your tranny shit or whatever. I don't care. You're not moving to the women's wing."

Bren McCool briefly considers this. The guard is probably right. This *is* probably trans shit. But it's also so much *more* than that.

They say, "No, like *this*."

And then Bren McCool spills out in an endless avalanche of white mycelial threads, through the letterbox-sized opening, up over the guard in a suffocating blanket. As the blanched bones of their supporting skeleton become entangled on the rim of the box, their sixteen fine, sharp, segmented legs emerge and rip the hole larger, like a knife in a rectum.

And Bren McCool is out.

MAMA IS A BUTCHER

WINTER HOLMES

IN AND OUT, the needle glided through soft flesh, affixing a new skin where the old had been removed. Riley winced at the stinging pull of the thread, but at fourteen years old, they were well used to it by now. Whenever they'd grown a few inches taller, the skin had to be replaced, and they were glad, once it was done, to wear a roomier suit, to have full range of movement back again. Even if they were always a little sore.

"Keep your eyes closed," Mama whispered. "We're almost done."

One last pull, and a quick knot.

"All set, darling. You look just wonderful."

Riley opened their eyes and looked at themself in the mirror. Of course, it was never really themself that they saw. Only a carefully stitched-on face would ever look back at them, beautiful and perfect and perfectly unfamiliar.

"I love it," they said. "Thank you, Mama."

Mama clasped her hands and held them against her mouth, smiling proudly.

The sun sat red and heavy in the sky when Mama called Riley to the front door.

"All of these," she said, pointing. "Can you take them to the corner? So the trash men can pick them up."

She'd piled bags and cardboard boxes on the ground, left over from deliveries of items she used in the business: twine, butcher paper, animal feed.

"Please? They make the shop look dirty sitting here."

"Yeah, sure," Riley said. "No problem."

The shop, and behind it their home and a small farm, were tucked into a grove and a long driveway led there from the main road. It took Riley three trips to carry all the bags and boxes to the end of the driveway and the heat stuck to them every step of the way, so that they were all sweat and ragged breathing by the time they'd finished the job. They stood for a while at the corner by the road, panting and feeling the sweat collect under their newly stitched-on skin. They'd hoped to keep themself a bit cleaner, at least for the first couple weeks, but they were sure now that they'd stink to fresh hell by the time they got to change their skin again. Summers were always the worst.

A breeze blew by, kicking dust up around them. They closed their eyes, listening to the rustling leaves, the wind in the wheat field across the road, the—

They heard a scream. "Stop!" A girl's voice shrieked in the distance. A boy's laugh. Riley hesitated for a moment, jaw clenched, before starting towards the sound.

"Give it back!"

A ways down the road, three boys passed a box around, weaving it just out of reach of a girl's desperate hands. The boys laughed as she stumbled and cried.

"Hey—" Riley's voice was quiet at first, then louder as they ran towards the group. "Hey!"

"Whoa." The first boy to see them, the tallest of the group, took a wide step back, gripping the box tightly.

Riley lunged towards it, but another boy gripped their shoulder hard, yanking them backwards. A tearing sensation, the sound of thread popping. Riley yelped as they hit the ground.

"Christ, Danny, did you just touch it?" the tall boy said.

"Shut up, I just saved you!" The boy who had pulled Riley down sneered.

"She said give it back!" Riley clutched their shoulder to ease the throbbing pain.

"Sammy, is this your new best friend?" One of the boys chortled, a smug smile on his face. "You better be careful. It's a cannibal, you know. Turn your back for a second and it'll eat you and wear your skin as a prize."

The girl stood between Riley and the boys, out of breath, brow furrowed. "You don't know what you're talking about!"

"Whatever," he said. "Besides, Danny's probably next anyway. It'll probably curse him for pushing it over. Sleep with one eye open tonight, bro."

Danny stuck his tongue out. "Man, screw you."

"Let's go." The tall boy threw the box down at the girl's feet. "This just got lame." He turned to leave, and his friends followed suit.

The girl snatched the box up and opened it slightly to check its contents, tears welling up in her eyes. She turned to Riley and offered them her hand.

"Are you alright?" She helped them up off the ground.

"Yeah," Riley said, dusting themself off. "I think they busted my shoulder, though. Is your stuff okay? What's in there?"

"It's my bird," she said, staring down at the box. "He died. I was going to the woods to bury him."

"How did he die?"

"I don't know. He was sick, I guess, when I found him a couple weeks ago. I tried to nurse him back to health. But it didn't work out."

"Oh, I'm sorry."

The pair stood in silence for a moment. Riley shifted awkwardly.

"I'm not a cannibal, you know."

"Yeah, I know. I know who you are. You're the butcher's kid."

"That's right."

"My dad says you're a freak. He says your mom says you're sick. I don't care what you are, because you saved my bird. I'm Samantha, by the way." She stuck her hand out at them.

Riley shook her hand hesitantly. "I'm Riley."

"C'mon, Riley, let's go bury him before it gets dark."

Riley blinked at the deep blue sky, the red sun just disappearing behind the horizon. "Isn't it already dark?"

"It's not dark 'till I can't see without a flashlight."

Riley laughed nervously, but followed her into the woods all the same.

"I think this spot is perfect." By the time the pair had found a spot Samantha was satisfied with, it really had gotten dark, and Samantha was carrying a flashlight she'd pulled from her back pocket.

They stood near the bank of a large pond, fairly deep in the woods, deeper than Riley had ever gone. They were still for a moment, watching fireflies dance above the water.

"This pond is pretty, right? It's one of my favorite spots." Samantha crouched down and started to dig a hole with a stick she'd picked up nearby. "During the day, the water's like a mirror. It's probably like that at night too, but it's dark so you can't see good. You mind helping me?"

"Oh, sure." Riley grabbed their own stick and started digging with her.

When they had themselves a small hole, Samantha opened the box and tentatively pulled out the body of a mourning dove. Wings held close to the body, eyes shut tightly, it looked as though it must only be sleeping, but for the insects crawling through its feathers, looking for flesh to feed on.

"I think you took good care of it," Riley said. "It looks like it died peacefully."

"Thanks." Samantha lowered the dove gently into the hole and pushed the dirt back over it slowly with her hands.

Riley sat against a tree and gazed out at the water. The pair sat in silence for a minute, but Riley could feel Samantha's eyes on their face, staring at them from her spot on the bank.

Finally, she broke the silence. "Why is your skin like that, anyway? Will it fall off if you don't stitch it on?"

"Um, it's not really my skin. It's from the pigs." Riley rubbed their shoulder, which still radiated a dull ache.

"Pig skin? Like, from the ones your mom chops up?"

"Yeah."

"Why?" Samantha's eyes were wide.

"Well, it's better if it's real skin, right? You wouldn't want to have some kind of fake stuff on you. Like plastic, or something. That would be uncomfortable."

Samantha frowned. "Who cares if it's fake or not? What happened to your own skin?"

Riley paused for a moment, but finally shifted closer to Samantha. "Promise not to tell anyone?"

"I promise." They were both whispering now.

"I'm not really human. I'm some kind of monster."

"No way!"

"It's true! My mama says I'm so horrible, if anyone ever found out what I actually was, I could no longer go on living. She won't even let me see myself." Riley sighed. "This skin is just here as a disguise. It's the closest I can get to being human."

Samantha rubbed her forehead. "So, then . . . you're, like, some kind of Frankenstein?"

"Frankenstein was the scientist, not the monster."

"So, your mom's some kind of Frankenstein?"

Riley laughed.

Samantha drew circles in the dirt with her finger. "I was surprised when you came to help me today. You never seem to leave the shop."

"I was surprised, too. I just didn't like seeing those guys

gang up on you like that, all by yourself. I guess I could relate to you, somehow. I mean, I've got my mom, but other than that, I'm all alone."

"You don't have any friends?"

"No . . . " Riley drew their knees in close to their chest. "I just freak people out, you know? And even if I could make friends, what would be the point? They wouldn't really be friends with me, they'd be friends with the disguise, with the person I'm pretending to be."

"I'll be your friend." Samantha smiled. "Not with whatever fake pig-person your mom wants you to be. I'll be friends with the real you, the scary monster who saved me from bullies and came with me to bury my bird in the woods, even though it was dark out. I want a friend like that."

Riley blinked. "Really?"

"Really."

"Okay." They grinned. "Let's be friends."

Riley turned to watch the fireflies. It really was quite dark out.

They looked back at Samantha. "Hey, what time is it?"

"Nighttime."

"No, seriously, I—" They jumped to their feet. "Oh god, I should get back home."

"Uh-oh." Samantha stood, brushing dirt off her shorts. "Here, I'll show you the quickest way out."

They stood at the edge of the woods next to Riley's home. Samantha took Riley's hand as they started to leave.

"Will you meet me again? By the pond?"

Riley nodded. "Yeah, can we hang out tomorrow?"

"Okay."

Riley walked home, guided by the yellow of the porch light, while Samantha watched from the trees.

Inside the house, Mama stood in the kitchen, peering

out the window. When Riley came in, she turned to them with frantic energy.

"There you are! Where have you been? I was worried sick!"

"I—" Riley felt a pang in their stomach at the thought of her finding out about Samantha. "I was just exploring the woods. Got a bit lost and, uh, it took a while for me to find my way back home. Sorry, Mama."

"Goodness sake, be more careful, child! You know it's dangerous just wandering around all by yourself."

"Yes, Mama. Sorry."

Mama gripped Riley's shoulder hard and kissed them on the cheek. Pain shot through them from the injury, but they kept silent. If they told Mama they were hurt, they'd have to tell her what happened, they'd have to tell her about Samantha. They hugged Mama goodnight and went into the bathroom.

Standing shirtless in front of the mirror, Riley inspected the wound in their shoulder. The thread had broken in one spot and the skin had loosened around it. They lifted the skin gently. Blood caked the inside, where the thread had torn through their flesh. They grimaced. They tried splashing water on the wound to clean it, but it stung and made them feel sticky, so they quickly abandoned the attempt and went to bed, hoping they would feel better in the morning.

They did not. Their throbbing shoulder woke them with the sun. But after helping Mama with the morning chores and wolfing down their breakfast, Riley gamboled off into the woods to see their new friend, the pain fading into the background.

"You're late." When they finally reached the pond, Samantha was hanging upside down, her knees hooked on a tree branch, her long hair dangling below her. Looking down at Riley, she squinted and crossed her arms.

"I got a little lost on the way here," Riley said. "And, hey, we never decided on a time to meet up."

"To punish you for this crime," Samantha jumped to the ground, "I sentence you to the dungeon!" She pointed confidently at a large pile of sticks.

Riley laughed. "Is that the dungeon?"

"Well, I was trying to build a fort earlier, but it didn't work out so good. Can you help me? If you help me, I'll lessen your sentence. Consider it community service."

"I shouldn't even have a sentence!" But they helped her anyway.

They played like that a lot in the following days, making things from sticks and leaves and catching frogs and bugs.

Insects are relentless in the summer. Because they wore a bloodless skin, mosquitoes had never really bothered Riley. But they spent much of their time by the pond batting away persistent flies.

They learned to ignore the ache in their shoulder.

Once, on a day when the pair both buzzed with excited energy, feeding off each other's amusement more than usual, Samantha followed Riley home where she normally would've waited in the tree line. Behind Riley's house stood a pair of metal barrels. For Riley, these barrels had long blended into the background of their every day, and they walked past them unseeing and unbothered. But when Samantha saw them, her eyes lit up with curiosity. She skipped towards them.

"What's in here?" She reached out to touch one.

"Don't touch those!" Riley barked. "We use those to dissolve the parts of the pigs nobody wants. It's acid, it's dangerous. Mama won't even let me touch them."

"The parts nobody wants?"

"Yeah, you know, like bones, innards and such."

"People don't use those?" Samantha's eyes flickered from Riley back to the barrels. She scratched her head.

"Nobody buys them. Mama says."

"Not even for, I don't know, soup?"

"Soup?"

Before they could continue, Mama flung the back door open, eyes wide.

"What's going on here?" Her brow furrowed.

Riley jumped. "Mama, I'm just talking to—this is my friend, Samantha."

"Samantha?" Mama breathed deeply, like she might yell, but her expression softened and she spoke quickly and quietly instead. "Samantha, honey, run along now. Don't you have to be home?"

"I guess so." Samantha hung her head. "It's getting around dinner time, huh? See you later, Riley."

Riley waved goodbye as Samantha made her way around the house, towards the trees and the long driveway. Mama pulled them inside.

"Is that girl the reason you've been out in the woods all times of day?" She leaned against the kitchen counter and glared at Riley, who shifted awkwardly under her gaze.

"Um, yeah, I guess. We've been hanging out."

"I knew you had to be seeing somebody. You've been acting different lately. Don't let this girl change how you behave around here."

"Mama, I won't, she's a good friend, she wouldn't—"

"I know her type." Mama wrung her hands and looked out the window. "She'll get you in trouble, if you're not careful. I don't wanna see her around the house anymore, okay?"

Riley looked at the floor.

"*Okay?*" Her eyes were daggers.

"Okay, Mama. Sorry, Mama." Riley shuffled slowly out of the kitchen.

"It's okay, dear. I just need you to be more careful," Mama cooed after them.

Riley stood on the bank of the pond. They had heeded their mother's advice, had spent less time in the woods with Samantha, but on this particular evening they were a bit moody and felt reluctant to leave their friend's side. They stared down at their reflection in the water. The face that wasn't theirs, Mama's perfect child, the freak, stared back up. They rubbed their shoulder.

"Does it still hurt?" Samantha leaned forward, trying to make eye contact.

"Yeah." Riley looked up at her. "That guy really messed me up. I thought it was just a cut, but it won't stop hurting."

"It's kind of been a while. Is it infected? It won't heal right if it's infected."

"Really?" Riley frowned. "Well, I don't know."

"It'll only get worse if it is. You should check it. Like, really look at it. You should probably . . . " She lowered her voice. "Well, I think you should take that skin off."

Riley gritted their teeth. "You know I can't do that."

"I'm sure your mom would let you if you're hurt, right? Can't you just tell her it's bad for you to—"

"Samantha, no!" Riley stepped away from Samantha and sat against a tree. "I can't. I don't ever wanna see myself without this skin. I'm horrible. I'm a monster."

Samantha sighed. "Well, I'll never believe that." She sat down next to them.

Riley pulled their knees up to their chest and rested their face in their arms. They sniffled, eyes focused away from Samantha's worried expression.

"You know," Samantha said, "I think our outsides reflect our insides. Even if most of the world thinks you're a monster, if you're good on the inside, the people that really matter will be able to see that. Your mom knows what you are, right? And she still loves you."

"She wants me to be different. She needs me to be something I'm not."

"C'mon, she's just looking out for you. I'm sure she'd love you either way." Samantha paused for a moment, thinking. "Look, I got weird stuff on my body, too. You're not the only freak."

She pointed to her arm, sticking it out for Riley to see. A dark mole sat splayed on her arm, five points sticking out in all directions.

"Don't it look just like a star?" Samantha said. "It's my favorite mole. My mom says it looks like cancer and I'll have to get it removed. But I'm keeping it as long as I can get away with it."

She snickered, and a small smile fought its way onto Riley's face, despite their attempts to remain somber.

"That's not the same at all," Riley said. "That's so small."

"Hey, I'm just saying we're all special in some kind of way. So you're just more unique than most other people! That doesn't make you bad." Samantha lay back in the grass with her hands under her head. "It's scary to see yourself for what you really are. That's true for anyone. But you said it yourself, what's the point of knowing anyone if they don't know the real you? Shouldn't that count for yourself the most?"

Riley watched the red clouds reflected on the pond.

At home, Riley swayed back and forth slightly, eyes darting around the room, trying to avoid Mama's gaze. She was quiet tonight, more collected in her mannerisms, but they had come home late and they could see the anger simmering beneath the surface, the suspicion piercing them through her eyes.

"Sweetheart, don't you know how late it is? I just want you to be safe . . ." she chastised them softly.

They wanted so badly to bid her good night, to escape to their bedroom and be free from the tension, but the pain eating away at them under their skin held them fixed, commanded them to speak on its behalf.

"Mama," they finally choked out, "I—well, I was wondering."

"Yes?" The sudden irritation in her voice grated on Riley's ears.

"Um, well, I . . . since I'm older now, you know? Maybe I can keep myself safe . . . Maybe I don't have to hide anymore."

Mama raised an eyebrow. "What do you mean?"

"Well, I, uh . . . maybe I can take the skin off."

"Oh goodness, no. No, no, no." Mama shook her head. "Why are you thinking these things? It's that girl, isn't it? She's why you came home late again, right? I told you she was trouble. She's putting these awful ideas in your head."

"Mama, no, I—"

"Don't you argue with me! I know girls like that. She'll build you up, have you thinking you're best friends, but when she gets you in trouble, and she will, it'll be you that has to clean up the mess. She'll leave you to fend for yourself. She wouldn't last one second with you if she saw what you really are."

Riley looked at the floor. "Sorry, Mama. I just thought . . . you know, even if no one else would accept me—even her—I'd still have you . . . right? Won't you love me either way?"

Mama brushed a bit of hair from Riley's face and smiled sadly. "Oh, sweetheart, I'll always wish the best for you, no matter what. But who could love a monster?"

The heat pricked Riley's flesh and they could feel sweat collecting in the folds of their façade. Their shoulder burned, pain like a dog gnawing on their flesh, and they rocked nervously. It had been five days since they'd last seen Samantha. Yet still they waited by the pond, hopeful that their friend would return to fill the woods again with laughter and bad jokes.

Riley stared at the pond with pouting eyes. Flies buzzed around their head. They swung an arm at them, but the flies held their ground, one finally settling on their shoulder. Forgetting their wound, Riley smacked it hard. Pain shot through their body. They yelped. The sound echoed through the trees.

Tears seemed to push at the back of their eyes, at the back of their throat. They swallowed hard and let out a shaky breath. A breeze pushed past them, but offered their concealed body no relief from the heat.

They frowned. Samantha was not coming.

Had she been scared off? Perhaps her imagination had gotten the better of her, perhaps even the thought of what Riley could really be had been enough to eventually deter her. But it was strange, how they felt now. So small, so frail next to the tall trees. The forest could swallow them alive and they wouldn't put up a fight. What a harmless thing they must have been.

Tears streamed from Riley's eyes, collecting in the stitched-down eyeholes in their skin. They sniffled and wiped their face with the backs of their hands, trying and failing to collect themself as they went in the house.

Mama was waiting for them in the kitchen, anxiously washing dishes. When they came in she dropped a plate in the sink, rushing to see what was wrong.

"Oh, sweetheart! What happened?" She brushed her thumbs under their eyes, wiping away tears.

"Samantha left me. She doesn't want to see me anymore. She's not coming back. She never even said why." Riley's voice cracked with emotion. "Not that she had to. I know why. I'm horrible. I'm disgusting."

"Oh, honey." Mama pulled them into a hug. "Don't say

those things." She sighed. "I warned you about her, I knew this is what would happen. They all leave in the end . . . this is what I try to protect you from."

Riley sobbed into Mama's shoulder. "I'm sorry, Mama. I didn't listen."

"It's okay, sweetheart," Mama said. "You'll know better next time."

Regret pushed down on Riley's head, and they struggled to stand against its weight, spending much of the evening hunched forward, staring at the floor. It pushed out from their heart, and Riley choked on it, thought it would suffocate them, clutched their chest in pain.

But when they looked in the mirror that night, Samantha's words echoed in their mind, telling them to take off the skin, to see their own face.

They went to bed in tears.

Twisting, writhing, fiery pain. Riley awoke with a start, their shoulder hot and sharp. They thought their muscle might crawl out from their skin. They ran to the bathroom, wincing, clutching their arm, and, removing their shirt, inspected their wound in the mirror.

They tucked shaking fingers under the loosened skin, the stitches still torn, and lifted it slowly to peer underneath. The wound oozed and stunk with rot. Riley's eyes widened as something flaxen and squirming caught the light. Turning, wriggling under the skin, maggots crawled through raw flesh, nourishing themselves on Riley's necrosing body. Riley screamed, stumbling backwards out of the room.

Mama came rushing into the hallway from the living room. "What's going on?"

"Mama, there's maggots!"

"What?"

"I have to take the skin off, you have to let me out! I'm being eaten alive!"

Riley gestured wildly at their shoulder and Mama bent over it, brow furrowed, looking over the torn stitch and the wound underneath.

She spoke quickly in a hushed voice. "Don't worry, honey, I've already prepared a new skin for you. We'll get you fixed up in no time."

Riley thought they should feel relieved, but their stomach turned at the news. Even rotting from the inside out would not have them freed from their disguise.

Riley squeezed their eyes shut, shivering slightly against the cool basement air on their naked body. They could hear Mama laying out their new skin, readying her needle and thread, pulling up a chair. Their wounded shoulder, freshly cleaned and stitched, still smarted, but it was a pain they were used to, a bearable pain.

"I'll make this as quick as I can," Mama said softly, and Riley felt her lining a piece of skin up with their forearm.

Riley clenched their jaw. The needle pressed through the flesh of their wrist, dragging the thread behind it. In and out. Their breath came out shaky. They heard Samantha's voice in their head:

What's the point of knowing anyone if they don't know the real you? Shouldn't that count for yourself the most?

What would be the harm of peeking? They already knew they were a monster, how could seeing it make it any worse? They felt Mama working the needle through their arm. They knew she'd be looking down. If they were fast, she'd never have to know.

Deep breath in. They cracked their eyelids open slightly, squinting down at the arm Mama was working on. Strangely, the first thing to come to their attention was not any part of their own body, but a detail of the fresh skin Mama was sewing onto them. A large, dark mole. Five points sticking out in all directions.

Don't it look just like a star?

Riley screamed, tearing themself away from Mama.

"What the hell?" Mama jumped up. "What did I tell you about—"

"What did you do?" Riley shrieked. "What did you do to Samantha?"

"Sweetheart, I—" Mama stepped towards Riley and they bolted out of the room, grabbing their clothes and running up the stairs. "Stop!" She yelled after them. "Come back!"

Riley ran through the house and into the shop, Mama chasing close behind. They fumbled with the lock at the front door. Mama grabbed their shoulder and they shoved her away, screaming.

Out the door, into the yard, around the side of the house. Mama following all the way. Riley swung around the back corner and smacked into a metal barrel. It toppled to its side with a loud crash, the lid coming loose, its contents spilling onto the ground. Riley hopped over it and started to run again, but stopped, giving it a closer look, their eyes going wide. Mama came around and skidded to a stop on the other side of the barrel, looking from it to Riley with pleading eyes. Riley's stomach dropped.

"Honey, please, it was the only way. You have to understand!" Mama cried.

Riley stepped back slowly. The smell filled their mouth and nose, choking them. Liquefying flesh, pink slop, acid and bone, running across the lawn. It wasn't pig. They should have always known it wasn't pig. From the end of the pile the empty orbits of a human skull stared up at them.

"People? This whole time, it's been people? Mama, why?"

"I had to make you human." Mama reached towards them, over the puddle of dissolving remains. "It had to be humans! Please!" She fell to her knees, weeping.

"Mama, I . . . " Tears welled in Riley's eyes. They gripped the porch railing. "I'm sorry."

Swinging their body hard, Riley kicked the second barrel. A crash, sloshing fluid. Mama raised her arms in front of her face as a wave of acid and flesh washed over her.

Screams echoed through the trees as Riley ran naked into the woods, crumpled clothes in one hand.

It wasn't until they'd reached the pond that Riley noticed how their feet stung from carrying them, bare, over sticks and rocks and thicket. They dropped their clothes in the dirt beside them and sat heavy on the bank, breaths heaving, humid air sticking in their lungs. They shook with adrenaline. They saw blood caked on their arm. At some point during the chase they had ripped Samantha's skin from their own. They felt a wave of guilt, as if the action could have hurt her more than she'd already been hurt.

It was then that their body, their real body, came into focus for the first time. Skin, blemished from lack of care, dull from lack of sun. A couple of moles, a dusting of hair. Puckered skin, scarred from years of stitches. *Human.*

Riley scrambled to the pond, bending over to see their reflection. Their same wide eyes, now coupled with a dark brow. Cheeks red with blood drawn to the surface from the heat. Sweat collected in the short hairs of their upper lip.

Their real face. Their living face. Their human face. Their life's greatest lie, dragged kicking, screaming, into the light. Their reflection warped and rippled as tears fell into the pond.

It wasn't a perfect body. It was chafed and scarred and bloody. But it was them. God, it was them.

FALL APART

GAAST

MY HANDS SHAKE as I finish stitching the fake skin to my latest doll. I peer at the stitches, drawing my face in close, but even with my glasses I can't quite tell whether I managed to stitch it straight. Sighing, I slump over the automaton. I feel like it all came so suddenly, as though one day I had steady hands, perfect acuity, sturdy elbows, enough muscles to lift my finished work—and the next day I had lost it all, my body utterly spent.

The cold automaton beneath me does not stir.

Tomorrow, I will have to lift the doll off of the makeshift gurney I now need to use to hold it and any other automaton I work on. I'll sit it carefully in a wheelchair and roll it out to the table, then desperately try to lift it into a regular seat. All before the family gets here, so they don't have to see. Each step is a risk; each moment a potential site for my body to fail. It wouldn't surprise me if some more brittle part of me snapped off, like a dead leaf.

For now, I pull myself to my feet and make my slow way upstairs. It's not late, no, but it's late for me, and I am of course exhausted. I grip the handrail and take the steps one at a time, watching my feet as carefully as I can. One slip. That's all it would take.

Sweating, I make it to my bedroom. My heart is racing,

but less with exertion and more with anger. A few years ago—just a few years ago—I would have scoffed at this. I would never have believed that I'd have to navigate stairs so carefully, manage my energy, worry daily about falling over. I'm not old enough to fall apart, but I'm old enough to rot. I still have so much more work to do. After all, I'm the only one who can do it. People need me and I'm willing to provide for them. I get to make these decisions, don't I? Not my body.

I sit heavily at my desk chair, just another grumpy old man.

In a few minutes, I've informed the family that everything is ready for them tomorrow, so please come in. I read through several other business emails, and though I want so desperately to fulfill their orders, I can't commit to them yet. Soon. If all goes well, soon.

That leaves the single new email in my personal inbox. It's from him, of course. I know what it'll say before I even open it, but I open it regardless. "Sure," he wrote, "so long as you share with me."

A tight smile stretches across my face.

Perhaps nobody makes me feel as old as he does. Nearly every time he emails me, he makes fun of me for being unable to use chat clients—their font is just too small—and tells me all about what he's been up to in his own time. He makes me feel so keenly the years of youth I spent apprenticing to automata makers, learning my craft; the years I was cloistered in workshops and seminars, he'd spent partying, enjoying life. He points out all my infirmities even as I try to skirt them; I point out his irresponsibility as others clean up his messes. Yet he always laughs, always, despite everything. Of course, he's in the same position I am. His body is also writing his future, and failure will come for him sooner than it will me.

I turn to look at the automaton set up lifelessly in the chair in the corner of my room. I made it in what spare time I could scrape together after I realized the direction my body was heading. I'm glad I had the foresight. In the past few weeks, as my joints and spine write litanies of pain, stretching the latest doll's production out twice as long as the previous one, four times as long as usual, I decided I was fed up. No more. No more.

In a quick reply I let him know I'll do it tomorrow, that I'll come find him soon. I won't get a response.

Finished, I drag myself over to bed. I still see some sunlight peeking through my window. I was always a night owl, able to work away until the early hours of the morning on whatever my latest project was. Now spring bright nights like these feel like jeers, mockery added to my self-deprecation. But I can't keep my eyes open. I can barely move. I have to sleep, like it or not.

When I wake, I feel just as tired as I did last night. But daylight is starting to stream in and heat the room; I try to shut it out, but my eyelids seem too thin to help me fight it off. Very well. I have to get ready before the family gets here.

It's a painstaking process, and it takes me almost two hours, but I manage to transport the automaton from the gurney in the workshop to a chair in the living room. The most harrowing step was the first: making the doll sit up was a complicated enough process, but lifting it from its perch to the wheelchair was terrifying. The doll's metal workings contributed to a significant weight, one I nearly buckled under. I also had to be precise, as the wheelchair is a small target to hit correctly with the bulk of someone's body, and I had to take care not to knock the chair around, all while almost falling over under the weight. One wrong *motion* could have sent me tumbling to the ground under the automaton, and though it's likely the family would have discovered me before long, who knows what damage my body would sustain in the interim?

I sit across from the doll at the table, waiting. All my joints ache. My bones do, too. I'm so tired. I can't understand it. I don't even feel like my arms are attached to me anymore, like at any moment they'll simply fall off. I fight off the urge to slam my fist down on the table in anger. What if I broke my hand?

But then . . . it wouldn't matter if I did, would it? Not in a little while.

A knock on the door shakes me out of my reverie. Did I fall asleep? Did I miss the family? I pull myself to my feet and shuffle to the door, letting a young couple with solemn faces enter. They both immediately spot the doll and look at each other. I can't see their expressions; I walk past them to the table and sit back down. They'll approach when they're ready.

Eventually, when they do, the father says, "We didn't expect her to be so—so lifelike." They stare at the doll, somewhat disgusted.

"We know it'll be *her*," the mother says, "but even still, there's something about . . . about it being so *real* . . ."

"Sorry. This must sound stupid," the father continues.

"Not at all," I say, gesturing for them to take their seats. "A lot of people say that they'd feel better if it looked just a little wrong, just a little more like an automaton. Sorry to be so blunt. But they want something a little more uncanny, just so they can remember that their child was once lost. They feel it's something they have to bear. They try to pay me extra sometimes to make something imperfect for them. But it doesn't work like that."

"It doesn't?" the mother asks. "Why not?"

I shrug. "The soul and the body grow in tandem. If you try to squeeze a soul somewhere it doesn't fit . . . "

The two hold each other closer. There's no going back.

They arrange their daughter's possessions around the table and on the doll. We close our eyes and I say a few words, calling her soul to us. Various presences flit through me, but only one makes the mother gasp. Yes, it feels right. I call out to her, asking her to take the hand of the doll wearing her favorite hat—and when she does, the doll's mechanisms start whirring and clicking, moving in jerky life.

Her parents cry out, finally reunited with their daughter. All three of them cry, even if the daughter can't shed tears. She was so young, but it means she has little trouble adapting to her new circumstances. To my surprise, her parents let her know quite clearly what has happened, why she's here, what she is now. Usually people save that for later.

Sometimes I wish this part of the process was harder or took longer. Shouldn't a séance take a painstaking hour? Shouldn't spiritual possession be a difficult, fraught process? Shouldn't death be harder to overcome?

As I watch the family walk hand-in-hand to their car to drive away from me forever, I burn with merciless envy.

I close the door, lock it, and face the stairs. I only need to overcome them once more.

Slowly climbing each step, I think on how I felt when the daughter started moving and her parents wept. That was joy I felt, briefly. That joy used to be strong enough to carry me through days, weeks, months. But now it lasts mere seconds. I'm the only one who does this. Without me, the joy this family felt will never be felt by anyone ever again.

Before I know it, I'm staring at the doll in my room. Our features are so fantastically different. I was always a little too plump, face a little too pudgy; he's lean and gaunt. My hair cascades down my back; his is short, styled just so. I compare my callused hands with his delicate ones, my hunched back with his straight spine. And all my wrinkles! What *is* a liver spot?

I laugh quietly. It doesn't matter, not anymore. I sit on the floor next to the doll, holding one of its hands. This one is some of my finest work. As soon as I told him my idea, he sent me a collection of the most perfect reference photos of himself. He seemed overjoyed to show himself off to me, to make me hate him even more. In return, I aimed for perfection, and I got as near to it as I possibly could.

Closing my eyes, I say a few simple words. The process

really isn't too difficult; much like a séance, you just need to invoke your own soul with the proper language, then make a simple request of it, something easy, like "enter the object I'm touching." It shouldn't hurt, but it does; in fact, it feels like I'm being torn apart, or rather like I'm tearing myself apart to fit into something much too small for me. It feels much like I'm ripping off each individual part of me, one by one, until all that's left is a pulsing mound of flesh and agony. The sensation is so unpleasant that it forces my eyes open just to make sure I haven't actually somehow destroyed myself completely, and when my vision clears I notice that I'm sitting in a chair, not on the floor, and that I can barely move.

It worked. I had assumed that the transfer would come with some odd sensations, just nothing so agonizing as this. But it's all spiritual; there's nothing wrong with my body, not anymore. I can move; I only *think* I'm experiencing unbearable pain every time I try to do so much as twitch, pain like I'm being compressed in a hot metal cage shaped to fit me exactly but one size too small.

I endure an attempt to laugh. I can overcome this. It's just like so many of the sleepless nights I wasted in workshops over the years: if I just work through the pain, I'll stop feeling it so acutely.

All I have to do is move. I do my best to stand up, hearing the mechanisms inside me spring to life and attempt motion; clenching my teeth, I do my best to forget the pain and lift myself in a single heave. I'm successful, but too much so; I can't catch myself before I fall over, landing face-first on the floor.

This is abnormal. Although many people have difficulty controlling their new bodies once they receive them, they adapt quickly. After all, the limited ranges of motion built into these automata helps them control their movements. Beyond that, the searing pain coursing through me is distressing—these bodies can't feel. I'm breathing heavily to fill lungs I don't have. My non-existent stomach churns. Every inch of my fake skin crawls and burns.

Slowly, I work on taking control of myself. I test out my legs, my arms, moving them from side to side; eventually, I bend my elbows and press against the floor, thinking through each and every step of the process of standing myself up. Each motion burns through me, my soul reacting for a body that can't. Taking this much painstaking control does nothing to help the churning sensation, the horrible inertia building up in my limbs, my head. I'm moving as though I'm not completely framed by mechanisms, like a fluid is building up inside of chambers lining my arms, legs, stomach, chest, head.

Using the wall to keep myself upright, I turn enough to catch sight of the body lying motionless on the floor of my room. That was once mine. I sneer at it. I'd kick it if I didn't think doing so would topple me over.

Of course, I have a minute or two to reverse things, to take it back before its brain is too damaged to continue. I stare at it and wait. I want to watch it decay beyond the point of no return.

By the time I'm satisfied that there's no going back, a sickening jerk tears through my shoulder. I careen forward, but I manage to keep myself upright. My fingers are twitching violently. I clasp them with my hand, but my body twists forward again, nearly lunging into the middle of the room.

I cannot describe to you the pain. My body isn't in pain; it can't feel. My soul is, and it feels all of these motions directly. Imagine taking something inelastic, something that has not flexed in decades, taking it with both your hands, and stretching it out, forcing it into a contortion, even slightly. Imagine that replicated hundreds of times inside of you, each little piece of yourself that you haven't thought about in years suddenly rising to the surface of your awareness. It's like all of my past regrets, all my memories of my family, all of my opinions on minutia—it's like all of these pieces of myself, on their emotional levels, are being forced into flexion after a lifetime untouched. It's like my soul, once whole, is now a writhing mass of maggots, and each wriggle is a nerve ending scraping against a knife. My head is perfectly clear, my body flawless, but my soul itself is in agony.

As I consider all this, my body jerks its way helplessly towards my laptop. I had thought that these motions were a reaction to my soul, simple interface errors causing my mechanisms to react, but no. I understand what I want to do as soon as I arrive at my desk. Taking my laptop in my hands, I heave it against the wall and watch it shatter into a rain of plastic and keys.

I'm no longer bound to that trash sprawled on the floor next to the chair.

No. Now I can take advantage of a timeless body. I can resume my work, just as soon as I regain full control of myself. Yes, all I have to do is keep working at it, fine-tune my machinery, and produce more dolls for more bereaved. I can keep going, keep helping families, keep doing what I've always done, yes . . .

Another violent jolt, to nowhere in particular. My whole body twists, leaving my head in a strange position. I lose my sense of where I am and topple over the bed. The sensation of a fluid filling my limbs surges further.

And if I can never regain fine enough control to do so? After all, transferring a soul into a vessel shaped unlike its original is a dangerous practice, one never done, one completely undocumented, save to warn against the doing. Who knows what will happen? What might become of my soul?

It doesn't matter, I think. I've chosen this freely. I escaped my fate already.

The woman who taught me everything I know about my work did so at the end of her life. She was rushing to teach me everything she should before was gone; she told me she couldn't sleep some nights, so worried was she that

I wouldn't master some fundamental aspect of our trade. Towards the end, she could hardly move, according to her—she was ambulatory, but she didn't have the motor control necessary to build dolls. She cursed herself for it.

So I asked her. I asked her why she didn't build a doll for herself to possess, to keep going as long as she wanted or needed. And she told me that, as valuable as she thought what we do is, she thinks that every soul should be allowed to be free. Death, she said, let souls take their true shapes, the shapes our bodies incubate them for.

My work is never finished.

Even now I can feel my insides stirring. I'm trying to move, but my body refuses. I feel like I'm liquefying. I laugh, dry and raspy. As soon as I do, I nearly choke. It feels like everything inside of me will spill out if I keep my mouth open for too long. Like my soul will escape and dissipate into the air.

I can't move myself, but my body is twitching. My fingers spasm, my arms flex, my legs pulse. The machinery inside me shudders and vibrates; I can hear parts moan and grind, metal scraping harshly against metal.

What's happening to me? What's happening? What I'm hearing and feeling—parts are shifting out of place, collapsing entirely, falling silent. Like I really am liquefying. If this body breaks, if I can't move, then I'll be completely trapped inside of it. Nobody will look for me. Whoever stumbles across me will find a broken machine. If I can't say the words . . . I can't move my soul anywhere else.

I hear a tearing sound, like ligaments severing. In tandem, my body jerks heavily sideways, and I fall off the bed. I can see myself, in all its malfunctions; my leg has split open at the shin, a long metal rod protruding from it. The rod twitches and moves, stretching itself out, feeling along the ground. It taps the floor, then keeps doing it, like it's thrilled to hear the noise, experience the resistance. I can't control it, but I can feel it, sensation coursing through it . . .

I don't feel pain, just the horrible jolts of my machinery as it shifts and grinds. I watch as the skin on my other leg seems to bubble, then split; another tearing sound as a second rod emerges. All over me metal contorts and whines. Nothing inside of me should look like those rods, but there they are, and more strands of metal are twining themselves around the rods, moving of their own accord to merge with what's emerged. Even my skull clatters violently, though of course I can't see whatever emerges from the top. My jaw, however, widens, the skin falling off completely; I can make out some shining metal mouthparts that clatter together of their own accord.

No, I can't close my eyes. Whether I'll end up with control over this frame at the end no longer matters to me. I'm excited. Excited to see what I'll become.

It takes all night. By the end of it, what's left of skin is simply hanging off of me in loose, torn chunks; a little on my spine, a little on my legs.

I can stand. It's a new way of standing, but it comes to me naturally. None of my legs feel unsteady, even if they terminate in points the same size as those slender rods that initially emerged from me. My ribs hang down off my spine, toward my knees; nothing remains between them, neither meat nor machinery. Just a hollow.

Ah, but it doesn't matter. I have more. A lot more. A set of arms, telescoping in stiff jerks. Horns protruding from my head, each granting me new means of perception. Clacking jaws, an elongated skull. I wonder where my teeth went? Are they what's lining my face, arranged like a hideous mask? And my fingers? Could they be waving atop my horns?

No, it doesn't matter. I have control of myself. A sickening, shining body, brass and austere.

I don't have time to admire it, however. I have a promise I need to keep. It's time to leave this workshop behind. To think, I was going to spend my life toiling here!

I don't need stairs, nor do I need directions. My horns

let me sense geomagnetism, let me see heat. I know where to go, how to get there. Why delay? In a few powerful strides, I launch myself at the window, shattering it, clattering heavily to the ground. I don't lose my footing, however, and gallop off.

I'm so much taller than the shocked, screaming people I pass. I've spent so much of my life hunched over, I never thought I'd see the tops of people's heads!

As I run (how wonderful to inhabit a frame with no need for air!), I realize that I don't know yet whether I can speak. Why not find out? I bellow the first thing that comes to mind, "I'm here!" The unnatural sound clatters heavily out of my mouthparts, completely without nuance, but it will do. I only need to speak a few words; after that, I'll never need to do it again.

He told me once, where he lived. And of course I remembered. It was so close to me, but in my old body I had no way of getting there. Another taunt—life lived so frivolously, so near to where mine was being wasted. But now, it's like nothing, traversed in mere moments. And I had no doubt that he'd be out there waiting for me.

He smiles as I approach, recognition in his face. "You look *great*!" he says, no sarcasm in his voice. "And this used to look like *me*?"

He walks around me, looking, enraptured. He runs his hand along my frame everywhere he can reach. His calm reaction makes other onlookers stop screaming—I'm almost disappointed by that. Other people approach carefully, calling out to him, "Hey, what *is* that thing?"

He looks at the approaching crowd, most of them still wary, some unsettled by how still I can stand. He grins mischievously. "I'm ready. Why don't you eat me, huh?" He strokes my mouthparts, or as much of them as he can from below.

I can't grin back, but as he touches me, I can grind out the handful of words I need, quietly enough that nobody hears. Just as his body is about to go limp, I grab it between my jaws and bite and chew, blood spewing everywhere as his bones splinter. The screams resume. Laughter bubbles up inside me, but it's not my laughter. My? No. How selfish of me.

Our former body, half eaten in our new mouth, a mess of ground flesh and cracked bone, slumps pitifully to the ground. It's a shame the blood isn't a deep black, or some kind of sludge; it looks just like normal blood, despite all its imperfections. Waste.

Ah, our other body, the one in the workshop bedroom. Another thing to crush in effigy. And once we've done that, we can go elsewhere and explore what it truly means to be us, the new us, the us we made, piece by piece.

How wonderful it will be to fall apart.

LADY DAVELINA'S LAST PET

CHARLES-ELIZABETH BOYLES

YOU REMEMBER GOING up the stairs to your apartment, tired and weighed down by grocery bags in each hand. That was your last memory before she took you: the stairs and your exhaustion.

But instead of taking you to your apartment, the stairs continued up and up. You didn't notice when you weren't carrying your groceries anymore; you didn't notice when you stopped climbing stairs and started just being in her room, but it happened. You were surrounded by her furnishings, flashes of gold and silver among fuchsia and cerulean, and a wall of mirrors that stretched from floor to ceiling but for their frames.

She was there, too, of course. For a moment you were stunned by her beauty: too tall, dressed in rococo finery, breasts like powdered quartz trembling above the neckline of her dress, and long, soft hands, decked with a single, tarnished ring.

From where she lounged on a striped chaise, she extended one of those hands to you, and mesmerized, you took it.

When you woke up, you were not yourself. You never would be again.

LADY DAVELINA'S LAST PET

You were a nacreous gel, you were a wolfhound, you were a seal, flopping across the floor. You were something different every morning. You were a deer, a hare, a squalling baby, and you endured it because when you did, she was kind to you. She would run one of those hands down whatever you had for a spine, and speak to you in a high, musical voice. You didn't understand any of the words.

The voice gave you hope: her tone was sweet, verging on apologetic. She spoke to you like she loved you even though you'd acted out, but really you were too shocked by whatever you had become to do much more than respond to any kindness she offered. You even dared to hope that she might help you.

That hope died the first time you awoke as a woman—the first and only time you cried. When you sat up in your little bed at the foot of her much larger bed, and saw your belly dusted with fine down where it had taken months of testosterone injections to grow hair, and felt the sleep-soft weight of breasts where you had worn your surgical scars with pride, you couldn't help it. You wept uncontrollably.

When you started crying, your breasts shook and pressed soft and smothering against your arms, and that only made you cry harder. The sobs were too high and too smooth. You glanced at the mirror and saw your body: utterly, classically womanly, much more so than you had been before you started your medical transition. You wailed, high and keening.

She stood over you, talking at you, her tone first cajoling and then harsh, less musical and more biting. You couldn't stop crying, couldn't stop looking at yourself in the mirror, your body a terrible, quaking dream of a beautiful woman, your face contorted, red and wet. She was yelling at you now, but you barely heard her over your own helpless weeping.

She smacked you then, an open hand across your hairless cheek. The pain was bright and instant, knocking you from your bed to the garish, black-and-white stone floor. In the mirror you saw your body, recurved, hip high and sloping disastrously to a waspish waist, breasts pillowing against each other, against your narrow ribcage. You gasped, ragged and hot, and shook with sick sobs.

She yelled something that sounded obscene, looming over you in the mirror. You cringed in on yourself, face still stinging, but your breasts were soft and heavy and when you curled up, they pressed against your arms and hairless chin. You even tried to stop crying, but you couldn't make yourself still.

So you were sobbing when she did something with her hands, too fast for you to see in the mirror, too blurred by your tears to take in. Still weeping, you felt your mouth shift, your teeth lengthening and almost biting off your tongue, your skin stretching against your jaw as you tried to make any kind of sound beyond a wretched, panicked snuffling, but you couldn't. Your mouth was gone, and the world that was the room went dark as your eyelids smoothed together like clay. When you touched your face, you found it wet and featureless except for your nose, and on the cold stone floor you cried yourself to sleep again.

When you woke the next day, a bird so long and spindly you could barely walk, your neck muscular and stretched such that you couldn't swallow, you felt only relief. She was cool to you, but you acquiesced to her whims. And when, days later, you woke again to a woman's body, you didn't cry or give her anything besides the affection she expected.

You couldn't have said how much time passed. The light changed from bright to dark, but you saw no lamps nor windows. You thought they were days, but who could say? Each one was an eternity, and then you slept and found the previous day had shrunk to a blur of alien sensation and fear. You woke in whatever form she had chosen for you; she gave you food to suit it; she sat on her chaise and beckoned for you to come to her.

Some days she wasn't there, but the food still appeared, ready to eat when you woke up. You ate it. It didn't occur to you until it was much too late that maybe you shouldn't have eaten it at all. The thought that you might be here forever sounded like a coin in a well: distant, muffled, and ultimately pointless.

Eventually, she gave you clothing, or at least, raiment suited to your form. When you were a dog, she'd tie a silk ribbon around your neck; when you were a goat, she'd fasten an embroidered cape over your back. The human clothes didn't fit at first. The trousers and jackets fell off, or dug in tight, painful in the armscyes and rises; corsets and gowns gaped taut between their lacings, or sagged at the neckline, hems trailing childishly. Like hers, the clothes were old fashioned, everything held together with ties and buttons and pins.

Your alien fingers fumbled the fastenings until the clothes started fitting, somehow. When she made you a girl, you dressed like her, and when she made you a boy, you buttoned your waistcoats with distant relief. Then she would beckon you closer and pet your hair and murmur and coo over you in that language you still couldn't understand.

One day—you were a bear, with heavy, shaggy limbs, your body soft and strong under dense fur but made a mockery by a frilly collar, the stone floor cold against your footpads—she took you out a door you had only barely noticed, and into another room.

You realized then, albeit dimly, that you had never left her bed chamber and that this must be her sitting room. While the bedroom was decked in candyfloss blues and pinks, the sitting room was upholstered in violet and teeth-aching orange, with scroll-footed sofas and tables carved like butterflies. Two other women, both also clad in dresses with daring necklines and absurdly lavish skirts, sat in the room, drinking yellow wine from glasses fine enough to shatter at a touch.

She sat on one of the sofas near the visitors, and beckoned to you as she always did. You went to her, snuffling along the checkerboard floor, and she petted your head and your spine, offering her hand for you to nuzzle. Her palm was soft against the sensitive fur and skin of your snout, and without thinking about it, you dared to lick her fingers.

"Davelina!" said one of the ladies, leaning back, fingers to breast, face a mask of delight, before letting spill a string of avid questions you couldn't understand.

She—your lady, *the* lady, Davelina—laughed like a flute trill, and with a gentle tap against your rump, she gestured for you to go to the visitors.

You let the visitors run their soft hands and long nails through your fur, ruffling your ears as if they thought you were beautiful.

⚧

It wasn't long after that that she took you further afield. She had begun to be more openly affectionate with you, as if she weren't trying for your favor but expected it. She would hold you on her lap, stroking whatever you had for a head, or climb up onto the bed and pat the counterpane expectantly until you climbed up next to her, where she would lay one heavy arm across your body, murmuring gentle sounds as the lace of her chemise scratched your back. Once, when you were a snake, your body thick and undulating in a way that would have turned your stomach if you'd had the stomach you expected to turn, she draped you around her shoulders and showed you to visitors again. They bent their powdered faces close to you, and you hissed and tickled their noses with your tongue, to their delight.

The first time she took you to the courtyard—you were

an old man, your joints swollen, your skin crepey and your hair flyaway gray—she led you past the sitting room, down what seemed like an endless hall of gilt, mirrors, and checkerboard floors. There were other rooms and other doors leading off the hall, but in between you saw yourself, your suit comically bright and close fitting, the satin a stark contrast to your wrinkled face, gnarled hands, and the pain of your every step.

You watched yourself, a stranger, so distracted that you scarcely noticed when you emerged from the long hall and into a courtyard bordered by an arcade. The light was a misty gray, and the lawn was covered in dense green grass dotted with spiral-trimmed topiaries. When you reached its edge, she gave you a gentle pat on the back, encouraging you to sally forth. She herself moved an arch or two down the arcade and took a seat on a bench, withdrawing a small book from a pocket in her voluminous skirts.

You took a few tentative steps into the grass. The ground was softer against your bare and aching feet than the stone had been, but the dirt beneath it was light and loamy, the give upsetting your balance. Unsteadily, you took a few steps more, still in sight of her, but you noticed that there was a fountain not much further in. You fixed your gaze on it, and flexed your core—the mercy of muscles you knew how to work, the pain in your knees and back—and made your way over to it. When you reached its lip, you steadied yourself with an aching hand, and slowly sat with your back to the water, your vision blurred with effort but nonetheless fixed on her.

You watched her reading, her face composed in an attitude of arch interest. You scratched your belly, and slowly unbuttoned your waistcoat. You took care that the tail of your coat didn't fall into the water, burbling delicately behind you. You wondered how long you had before you would need to piss, wondered if she would berate you for pissing in the fountain. At least you had that option, wracked though your body was.

Something flashed in your peripheral vision, and before you could make sense of it, from the half-misted courtyard—it seemed as if there were a ceiling, but when you looked up, you couldn't see it—a red hart trotted over to you. His body was as long as yours, his antlers three-pronged and crawling with velvet, and seated on the edge of the fountain, you could barely see over his shoulder. When he dipped his head to you, you almost fell back into the water.

"Who are you?" he asked, and the shock of his throaty and trumpeting speech hit you before you realized: you had forgotten your own name.

"I—" your voice rasped from lack of use, creaked in aged vocal folds, "I don't know."

"Well, that's bad," said the hart. He folded his legs and sank into a dignified lounge. "How long have you been her pet?"

"I don't know," you said again. Your voice whistled unfamiliarly as some distant part of you scrambled to recall the name you had chosen, had sweated over and introduced and reintroduced to all those people you used to know. You didn't even remember what it had replaced.

"Well, you ought to figure it out," said the hart. He yawned and shook his head, his antlers passing dangerously close to your face. "Hers don't last long."

"What—wait, 'hers'? What do you mean?" Your voice came easier, though it still sounded alien to you: it was an old man's voice, and you were still in your early thirties.

"Her pet. Think she dressed you up for fun?" asked the hart, with something like amusement in his voice. "She runs right through them."

You glanced over at Davelina, where she sat by another woman in an equally-overwrought gown. She looked up at you and smiled.

"My name's Ray, and I was human once, too," said the hart. He winked at you. "That's my lady, over by yours."

A finger-snap: she summoned you.

"Here," said the hart, rising from where he lay. "Put your hand on my back for balance."

With Ray's assistance, you made your way over to where the ladies sat. When they saw you, leaning on Ray, trying not to clench your hand in his smooth but prickly fur, they gave each other twin looks of delight and beckoned the both of you with more urgency. When you reached them, the ladies petted and stroked you and Ray both, running their hands down the hart's strong, thick spine, and pinching and patting your sagging cheeks until you felt sure you had a bruise.

You were a thick-shelled crab, you were a bristling boar, you were an owl, and when you flapped your wings, you almost knocked over the table by the chaise. But meeting Ray had awakened something in you. Something in you was pushing past the shock of it all; something in you was noticing patterns; something in you was planning for escape.

She usually put you back in some human form before leaving you for a while, but did so without regard for what might be comfortable for you. You white-knuckled your way through days as a crone, as a girl—the girlish days were better, because at least then your body was young and didn't hurt as much. Once she left you as a burly young swain, muscular and blandly handsome, but you found you missed the soft flesh of a belly that felt familiar more than you enjoyed the by-then-shopworn novelty of having a penis.

You knew she was getting bored of you because before she did, you would spend a day as a sort of gelatinous mound, opalescent and quivering, crawling stickily across the stone floors. On those days, you wouldn't get—and didn't need—food or clothes. Eventually you greeted the days of being a dense mucous with relief, because it meant you would be alone. Not that you did anything: the books were unillustrated and filled with writing that swam when you looked at it, and there was little else you could reach that interested you. It was just nice to be alone.

When you were an animal, you noticed that your thoughts were fuzzier, your sense of time distorted. But you learned to move as a snake, an alligator—the heavy power of your jaws tempted you to violence, but you didn't want to be an alligator forever—and even to fly a little. You never found a ceiling when you flew, but couldn't shake the sense that you were inside some vast structure where celestial light couldn't penetrate.

Almost by accident—who knew how long you'd been there, who knew who you'd been before?—you learned, too, how she worked her magic on your body.

You had awakened to a body that felt more like home than the others. Just a guy, about the right age, about the right height and weight. Something about the hair was off—you had never managed to grow a beard, you didn't think, and now you had a dapper little van dyke and a robust mustache. She had laid out a handsome suit for you: bright, sharply cut, and dashing. You allowed yourself to preen in the mirror, admiring the curve of your leg in the close-fitting breeches, the way the jacket displayed your thick torso and powerful shoulders, the elegant peak to your hairline.

But you saw her face reflected, the look of vague dissatisfaction. Her brow creased, and you chanced to notice that she moved one finger over the ring she always wore, with its tarnished silver band and dark stone that flashed a brilliant teal.

If you hadn't been looking for it, the touch of the ring would have vanished from your mind in the flood of disappointment that followed. You felt your flesh begin to move, fat and muscle doing alchemy under your skin. A moment's incredible pain in every pore as hair ungrew in places and sprouted out in others; a cold, wet, orgasmic sucking as your genitals rearranged. As you watched, your chest and hips strained fast against your clothing, your limbs contracting painfully as muscle and bone shrank by inches before your eyes. With a sudden, intense ache in your sinuses, your nose shrank and tipped up at the end, your jaw rounding and softening as your lips grew plump and pink.

Within moments, you were a short, fat woman in clothing made for a taller man. Before you had time to think, just barely enough time to bite the inside of your lips to keep from crying in dismay, she pointed to your bed. A fine dress and undergarments were already waiting for you.

Your shirt, when you tugged it off, tangled in your hair, glistening curls that brushed your buttocks. You nearly fell as you stumbled from your breeches, the knee buttons too tight over your legs. In off-balance glances, you took in the high, narrow crease of your waist, the drift of flesh across your pelvis and your hips, your delicately down-sloping shoulders and heavy-hanging bosom.

In the dress—and chemise, and corset, which she helped you lace with deft fingertips—you looked at yourself, and knew you would have worshipped the ground you walked on if you had been looking at anyone but you. As it was, your feet and hands were so soft and dainty you worried they might be prone to swelling. She smiled at your reflection and touched you on the shoulder, moving you towards the door.

There were guests in the drawing room, fine ladies and gentlemen. They petted you and twirled your hair and spoke in nonsense to you. You pretended delight in their attention more easily, though, because now you knew how Davelina made you every morning and unmade you every night. That power rested, it seemed, in her darkly shining ring.

You saw Ray again. He had been a man once, young and dispossessed, when his lady had stolen him, and he told you what little he knew of the pet you now were. Though you couldn't always respond, you learned that her pets wore out quickly, their bodies exhausted by the frequent changes to which she subjected them. Or so Ray guessed.

"Did you figure out your name yet?" he asked each time you saw him.

The first time, you were an octopus. Your beak couldn't have formed words even if it weren't pointed towards the ground, and using so many limbs to move required a lot of thought. Your nerves were on fire, and the grass of the courtyard tickled your sensitive suckers. Besides, you still didn't know.

The next time, you were an overgrown magpie, and could only nod, shake your head, and cackle raucously. She hadn't let you fly to the courtyard, presumably to avoid you breaking things; hopping all that way had exhausted you down to your bones. You had given up trying to remember it, so you shook your head and, shamed less by Ray's demeanor than by your own deficiency, pecked helplessly at the grass and dirt.

Both times, he nudged you gently with his snout, and said, "It'll come to you," in as soft a voice as he could manage. He talked instead about things he remembered: skateboards, and kissing boys, and cars and cell phones and cheap, bad coffee. As if remembering a dream, you remembered them too, and it was a comfort to know that you had not always been her pet, your body had once been your very being, you had seen the sun and stars.

Finally, you saw him again when you were a man, tall and sick-thin, your ankles and knees knocking together when you walked, your laryngeal prominence moving by inches whenever you swallowed. You felt ill and weak, and again you sat with difficulty on the lip of the fountain, your pelvic bones brittle against the stone. You wondered whether what Ray had told you about the body wearing out with so many transformations was already happening, or if she had just wanted you to be sick. Your tendons felt baggy, your guts unquiet.

But when Ray trotted over to you and asked again if you had figured out your name, you nodded.

He pulled back. "Can I know it?"

"Meno," you said. Your voice was wrong, resonating in your nasal cavity and rattling your bony chest. You didn't know where the name had come from. Like the voice, the name wasn't quite right, but it would do.

Ray smiled, a gesture so strange on a hart's face you would have laughed if you didn't recognize it.

"It's a nice name," he said. He nuzzled your hand, and then folded himself to the ground to rest his great head on your wasted lap. You bent forward—you could feel all your bones, and you had so little flesh—to speak as close as you could get to his soft, velvety ear.

"She uses a ring," you whispered. "If I can get it from her, I'm going to run."

"If you run," he said, peering at you with big, dark eyes, "call my name, and I'll run too."

"I will."

"Promise?"

"Promise."

A snapping of fingers, a clicking of tongues. You were summoned back to your ladies, the two of you together, but the promise you had made hung heavy and joyous in your heart.

You were a maiden fair, a slug with cilia-feet and eyes on swiveling stalks, a boar with prickling mane and heavy tusks. You waited, watchful, but she wore her tarnished ring, flashing dull or bright, at every waking moment.

The constant transformation was taking its toll. You found it difficult to sleep, instead lying awake, waiting for the change, startling out of slumber as your flesh and skin and whatever you had for bones moved and shifted.

You were a frog, a mare with flashing eyes—but when you're lucky, you're very lucky. You wake up in the night to a somnolent quiet, and you're close to what you used to be: a man with thick limbs and a soft paunch, your hair still wild from your troubled sleep.

You are used, by now, to rising silently from your little bed, to stretch what you can stretch when your nightly transfiguration renders you too stiff or loose to sleep. Usually, she is sitting up on her chaise or in her bed, watching you. This time, though, she lies with her eyes closed, apparently fast asleep.

To see if she's pretending, you knock a book from a table. It lands on the floor with a flat slap, but she only lets out a little snore and shifts beneath the counterpane in response. You almost laugh, but instead you inhale deep into your belly and creep over to the side of the bed. With a slow exhale, you snatch the ring from her finger.

She twitches, snorts, but doesn't wake. You back away, gaze shifting towards the door, and slide the ring onto your finger. With footfalls that feel loud but make no sound, you hurry to the door.

Before you have a chance to think, the doorknob is in your hand, and you are opening the door just enough to slip your body through the gap. But the ring slides on your finger, and in your attempt to keep it on, you lose your grip on the door. It falls shut behind you with a loud and echoing *thunk*.

You freeze. You hear a murmur from behind the door, a shift of bedclothes, a harsh cry. You run.

The door slams open behind you as you scramble through the sitting room, hip-checking one of the more delicate tables in your haste. It crashes to the floor as you pelt through the door into the long hall lined with mirrors.

"Ray!" you scream, and your voice sounds almost right in your head, your body feels almost right as you run hell-for-leather. You hear her behind you, her own feet slapping against the stone, but you don't stop. The hall is long and blessedly straight in the dim light that passes for night in this place. Doors slam open behind you, before you, but you run full tilt into the courtyard. You hear hoofbeats and a trumpeting call, both coming from somewhere near, but you can't afford to stop. You glance back, and she's rounding the corner into the courtyard behind you.

"Ray!" you call again, as you dodge topiary and fountain and dive through another door on the far side of the courtyard into an unfamiliar hall. This one is lined not with mirrors but with swords and shields, the light now the flickering red of torchlight though you see no torches or sconces for them. You barely avoid falling down the stairs into a stepped bath, and instead dodge around the outside of it. You're winded, and she's so close behind you.

The hooves resound again, and when you glance back, the red hart is stuttering to a stop just at the edge of the bath. Ray lets out a trumpeting bellow, but before you can escape with him, she has appeared in the door.

Her hair is mussed from sleep, and her chemise floats around her as she comes to a halt. She seems even taller than before, almost filling the doorway. The ring twitches, too big for your finger, and you push it into place, thinking only that you want her gone.

She screams at you again, and charges towards you, leaping impossibly across the bath, but as she hurtles towards you, you feel your body changing. At first you think it's nausea at your own impending demise, but then you feel your thoracic cavity swell and grow hollow as your ribs creak and turn down. You see the skin of your belly split open into a gaping, ragged mouth, and spikes thrust up from your pelvic bone. A looped tongue of your writhing intestines spills out of the maw. You scream, and almost slip on the steps of the bath, and then she's on you.

But then she's in you, and your torso spasms forward, bone ripping into flesh, jarring against bone—first hers, then yours. You lurch forward again, and her head is mash in the maw you've made, her hair catching on your pelvic teeth and cutting into your belly's gory lips. You spasm again, and one of her arms falls dully to the stone floor, sliding down into the water. And then you force her in as you're wracked by one last back-breaking bite, right through her spine, and her legs, heavy and dead, splash down into the bath.

For a moment, there is silence, only the lapping of the water, the arhythmic drip of blood from the maw in your belly. You look back at Ray, who stares at you with grave, cervidean eyes. It seems as if he's about to speak, but before he can, you pass your finger over the ring again.

It hurts so much you almost fall into the bath, where her dead legs marble the water with blood. Your ribs ratchet back into place, spiked teeth crunch back into smooth pelvis, skin flows against itself over muscles braiding smoothly back together. You feel sick, but it's a sickness that you know. When you sink to the ground and vomit, the burning bile and abrasive chunks feel like a homecoming.

"Meno," says Ray, when you fall still. He nudges your shoulder with his snout. "We have to go."

You nod and rise to your feet, your limbs shaking and bones throbbing with what you've done to yourself. You waver, and Ray kneels. You climb onto his back, his fur prickling against your groin and the insides of your thighs, and he bolts from the room as running footsteps sound from the far hall.

It feels like you barely blinked, but with a solid, final slam of a door, Ray has carried you out—really, truly, out. The two of you have arrived in a field of wildflowers, lit by a low, full moon.

"We can find a way back, I think," he says. "I've heard that you can."

"I know," you say.

"We can't stop for long," says Ray.

"I know," you say.

Nonetheless, you slide from his back, and together, you look up, into the unbounded depths of the heavens.

IN THE GARDEN OF HORN, THE NAKED MAGIC THRIVES

HAILEY PIPER

NEVER BUY MAGIC at a yard sale. Common knowledge Reza already knows when she starts fingering the crystals and geodes and other shiny rocks down the lengthy wooden table crackling under summer sunshine. Idle fingers make decent a cover: *Don't mind me, just looking around, not eyeing anything in particular*.

But she knows exactly what she wants. Common knowledge, no yard sale magic, fine, but where else might a lucky passerby parse through junk and find a dream? Reza had no particular treasure in mind when she first arrived, but two minutes on the grass and she's spotted genuine magic in the house's shadow.

She forces herself to take slow steps, browse a little, pretend she only stumbles upon the idol when her hand at last settles beside it.

Like the yard sale tables, its surface crackles with sunshiny warmth. It's a wooden shaft, sixteen inches long, as thick as her forearm, with coiling tree knots and column-shaped lumps growing down its sides. One end is jagged, broken off; the other narrows into a curved silver tip.

"Neat tchotchke," Reza says to the homeowner behind the table. "How much?"

"That thing?" The yard sale man scratches his head. He is aged and world-weary, but no chaos magician, only an accumulator of too many odds and ends. "Might look good over a fireplace, right? Fifty bucks."

Reza haggles him down to forty. If she tells him the truth, he won't believe it. And if he would believe, he'd never part with anything so priceless.

Whatever it is.

The front door opens a couple hours after Reza arrives home with her prize, still mid-research when her boyfriend joins her.

"Anything good?" Carver asks.

"Good is immeasurable, babe," Reza says. She sits cross-legged on the floor, the idol stretching over her thighs, laptop balancing on her feet. "Definitely a thing."

Carver squats beside her, a smirk splitting his black goatee. "Kind of a big dick, huh?"

"Not at all; this is average size." Reza strains to keep a straight face before bursting into laughter.

Carver kisses her cheek and starts to stand, but Reza grasps his arm. If she lets him go, dinner will follow, the next step in their morning, work, home, dinner, television, bedtime, sleep, morning cyclical routine. His guitar gathers dust on the wall and his paintings stare down in expectant judgment as Reza pulls him into a deeper kiss.

His lips pantomime intimacy, heart not in this. Best to let him go. Affection strains at every turn of their repetitious wheel. Jokes, work, and meals will only grease their daily journey for so long. For how much time can the wheel spin the exact same way before it flies off the axle and sends them crashing into a broken future?

Carver is asleep when Reza identifies her find. Internet searches rarely offer details for most genuine magical artifacts, lost in digital ravines, but traces of legend persist as if demanding to be known.

Reza strokes her palm over the idol's knotted shaft. "You, my friend, are an idol of love."

Carver must have been on the money, and Reza can't deny her prize has a phallic quality. Not that she's choosy; beggars can't afford it. Her interest in genuine magic forever aims at improving her life, in any possible way. A now-broken locket let her take ownership of this house two years ago, for example, and there is always more to gain.

What kind of magic can the idol offer? Reza finds no info beyond some spiritualism group who showed off the prize decades ago and then vanished.

The idol of love might double for fertility. Could Reza bear a god's child? Wouldn't her OBGYN be surprised if she waltzed into her annual pelvic exam tomorrow morning, pregnant by divinity?

Or maybe the idol can heal Carver's heart. He came out to Reza on their second date, long before moving in together, and she thought any matters troubling his body and mind to have been settled long before they met. She only knew she loved this shy young man with a wicked smile whose calloused fingers used to ache across paintbrushes and guitar strings.

But over the past year, those fingers have been idle, unwilling to touch paintbrushes, guitars, or even Reza. Carver speaks little, but she finds him eyeing his body sometimes, wondering at surplus of womb and lack of member with intensity she's never seen before. Who's harassed him? Who's revived ancient dysphoria? She doesn't ask, afraid the culprit might be Carver himself. Her affection has lost meaning, same as his hobbies of painting and guitar playing, everything draining down a hole in his heart.

Chaos magic offers a chance to patch over that

depressive spiritual wound. Therapy of the regular and hormone kinds have limits, but magic might lead his heart back to Reza.

Desperate tears slither down her cheeks, and she wipes them fast. The wrong fluid might confuse the idol. Most magic needs a thicker substance, and Reza has an inclination to what this one might drink.

The idol's silvery head gleams beneath the living room's moonlit picture window as she rolls her jeans off, chased by her panties, and then leans against the couch with her legs bowed wide. Her front teeth bite her lower lip to bleeding, and then she licks the idol's head, wetting it with blood and saliva.

"You do right by me, you hear?"

She grasps the idol's shaft by knot and lump, and then she slides the silver tip between her thighs. There's no helping a muffled scream behind bitten lip, but at least the pain is brief.

⚧

The fertility clinic office sits inside a joyless lump of gray brick, meaning the throng of two dozen scarlet-robed people stick out in the parking lot when Reza arrives the next morning. Their numbers swell in uncertain genders, varied skin tones, hair of every color, style, length. Some are older, or younger, larger, smaller, bonier, softer, more masculine, more feminine. Their robes flow from torso and limb, dancing with the wind.

These people don't belong outside small-town medical offices. Where is their big city, their stage?

"O gift of blood, we taste him again," a dry voice says.

Reza tries not to look again as she locks her car and makes for the glass sliding doors at parking lot's edge, but out the corner of her eye, she notices the scarlet-robed people turn their heads together as if bound by unseen wire to a giant puppeteer's finger.

"That idol of love, too phallic to be true, is the broken horn off a god's member," one of them says.

Another laughs before adding, "He has strolled long without it."

"O love-starved fool," the tallest of them bellows. "You've bled upon grand and forgotten power, and in unpracticed hands, it is a stranger with strange magics."

Reza reaches the sliding glass doors and hurries through, purse clacking beside her. She hammers her finger on the elevator's call button. None of the robed figures join her in waiting.

But a glance at the parking lot says they're all watching.

Reza has been called for her appointment when the idol's gift strikes.

She's getting up, getting this over with, and she only notices the zipper of her jeans has opened a moment before an inner quake buckles her at the waist. Clamoring voices overtake the crinkling of magazines through the clinic waiting room.

"What's wrong, honey? Cramps?"

"Is she going into labor?"

"She doesn't look pregnant."

"Charlotte, do you have a pad?"

A red-haired figure approaches with a plastic square—someone named Charlotte? Reza doesn't know. The tremor of an almost-orgasm rocks between her legs, except it's reaching out like a wanting hand. She's never felt anything like this before.

Charlotte flinches back, dropping the pad. Her face has gone pale, but no one's looking at her. All eyes fall to Reza.

And the panty-coated bulge pressing between zipper teeth. Reza's mouth trembles open, readying to scream.

Charlotte gets there first. "You're one of them," she says, thrashing an accusatory finger at Reza. "One of them!"

Reza doesn't know what she means. A chaos magician? How could anyone know that? She dashes from the waiting room to the elevator, taking the descent to zip her jeans. She then barrels across the parking lot, empty of its scarlet-robed throng, and into her car. The doors lock. She tries to breathe.

Unseen flesh stiffens in her pants. Aching, hungering, dancing on tender nerves. She pries her waistline up to look for evidence of her usual labia, where last night an idol of love had kissed between her thighs.

A phallic shaft now towers from dark hair, as if the fresh penis has fused and devoured existing tissue to create itself. The new flesh throbs against Reza's clothing. She wants to shout that this is impossible, but who is she to talk? She's the one who fucks with magic.

Can she call it impossible if magic fucks back?

"I know it was you," Reza says.

She stands in her living room, judged again by Carver's derelict guitar and paintings as she turns the idol in clumsy circles. Her hands examine every knot. Genuine magic means there is always more to gain, but Reza used to think the boons would always be gifts she wants. Here is a gift she needs to return.

The idol bears no obvious sigils, nothing to suggest magic carved by human hand. Reza can peel the wood, maybe find secrets carved beneath the surface, but to damage the idol might taint its power. No fixing her then.

Her fingers are busy searching the silver point for runes when it jabs her palm. Like last night, the idol is anointed in blood.

"Is that what you need?" Reza asks. "Fine then." She strokes her now-bleeding hand down the shaft and then raises the idol overhead. "I pray to the god of the idol, as old powers give and take, you have granted me flesh, and I wish that flesh returned."

Reza waits to feel a relieving tremor, for the pressure to vanish from between her legs, any sign of magical undoing. A pulse aches against her jeans.

Nothing has changed.

Of course. What self-respecting god would answer a vague title like *god of the idol*? Does she expect him to incarnate in flesh over weak cries for help? Divinity demands better. She remembers the scarlet-robed throng mentioning a horn broken off a god's member, but which god?

Reza needs a name if she's to undo this curse.

The yard sale is over, only trampled grass lying where tables once held cardboard boxes of junk and treasure, but the man who sold Reza the idol sits on the porch. He holds a whittling knife in one hand and a small block of wood in the other. It's beginning to resemble a duck.

Reza clomps up the porch steps. "Do you remember me?"

The yard sale man pauses his whittling and glances at her. He has the face of someone lost, and the scent of wood and dust around him suggests he's been rooted in this spot for some time.

Reza can pretend-polite her way through cramps, cuts, and all kinds of pain, but a magic pressure thrums below her waist, a raw inside now spilling out like intestines exposed to the air for the first time. She has no patience today.

"That idol you sold me belonged to a god," Reza snaps. "Do you know which one? Where you got it from? How to fix what it does?"

The man's head shakes back and forth at a glacial crawl. "I can refund you with proof of purchase."

Reza makes to tear her hair out. This is hopeless. The man has never known or believed in magic; he thinks he sold her an odd tchotchke, nothing more. One reason you never buy magic at a yard sale is lack of legacy. Where the magic comes from and what it means become forever unknown qualities. The scarlet-robed throng outside the clinic offered more knowledge in sixty seconds than this man will know in sixty years.

Reza is about to storm off when the pressure in her pants echoes at her hand.

Her fingers flex and strain. Flesh withers from them, the skin turning translucent with veins and pink tissue. Muscle converges in a fleshy star at her palm's center, where the hooded pink helm of a new penis surfaces from the idol's latest wound.

Reza's voice shatters into a feral shriek. No, not another one, not there. She wrestles the whittling knife from the yard sale man's hand and scrapes the blade down her palm, skinning hand-flesh and phallus-flesh alike. The still-forming member drops onto the porch in a bloody puddle. Veiny roots spring from its severed base and dig into the boards, feeding the shaft until it finishes transmogrifying. A coiled amalgamation of pink tissue and splintery wood now juts from the porch.

The man shouts something Reza doesn't catch. She's already dashing down his porch steps toward the street. He can't help her, no one can. She stops to tear her jacket off and bundle it around her hand. Mangled and bloody, but at least there's no phallus growing from the palm.

Had she not paused, the dark blue sedan screaming onto the lawn would have smeared her across the grass.

Reza staggers back from screeching tires. She's stammering, shaking, yet excited below her waist, blood and muscle almost screaming with excitement. Why would any part of her enjoy this? She blames the god, and his idol.

And Charlotte, who emerges from her sedan. "It's you!" she cries. "It's you, it's you!"

Reza reels back and jabs the pilfered whittling knife into the sedan's passenger-side tires. She then skirts around the back before Charlotte can reverse and crush her skull. Reza dizzies as she hops into her car and slams the gas. In a blink, she's down the street, making one turn, another, anything to at least escape Charlotte because there's no getting away from the catastrophe in her jeans and the agony in her hand.

How long has Charlotte been following? Would she drive on two flats to chase down her prey?

Reza doesn't want to find out. She makes another dozen zigzagging turns through town and only stops when she reaches the old movie theater, where she parks to sob over her steering wheel. Her jacket now runs red. She should go to a hospital, but after the clinic incident, she worries more people like Charlotte might come hunting.

Flesh swells inside her pants. What the hell does this thing want? Does it even know? Or is it after anything it can gain, the way she's been hunting any magic in reach? She can't be blamed for that after magic has seen her through hard times when the mundane world has failed to love her. Why torment her now? Carver's lack of affection for her might have nothing to do with any hole in his heart and instead seep from a universe that's now marked her as unworthy of love.

Reza feels eyes on her. She checks her rearview for Charlotte's sedan—nothing—and then glances ahead, where the scarlet-robed throng from this morning now haunts a narrow alley between the theater and a smoky-windowed mattress store. Their heads poke almost comically around the corner, curious and guarded. Reza tears out of her parking space to reach them.

"What do you want?" she snaps through an open window. "What do any of you want?"

But when she reaches the alley mouth, she finds it empty.

Heading home feels like giving up, but Reza has nowhere else to go. She locks herself in the bathroom, where she disinfects her palm, bandages it, and swallows double the recommended dose of painkillers. By the time she's finished with another bout of crying, Carver is home.

"Sweetie?" He reaches for her still-damp face as she emerges from the bathroom. "You okay?"

What else can she do? She tells him. And she shows him.

"All that from breaking the skin?" Carver asks. He's sitting on the floor, stroking the idol as if it's a beloved pet.

"From blood," Reza says, seated on the couch above. She's changed into sweatpants, which eases some of the pressure between her thighs. "I couldn't find out anything else."

She would take a machete and strip the idol layer by layer if she thought interrogatory violence would bleed answers. And if she had a machete. What will this transformation mean for her period? Will the penis bleed menstrual tissue? Or has the idol leeched at those organs to grow this dick, the way another ate first from her hand and then from the yard sale man's porch? She flexes her fingers—the skin is tight, but the ache has eased.

Fabric crumples. Reza looks up to catch Carver lowering his pants and boxers. "Babe?"

"One second," Carver says, bracing the idol. He chugs deep breaths in and out, and then he draws the idol's silver tip between his thighs, into a thick nest of black hair.

"Carver!" Reza snaps.

The pain is brief; she knows this from experience. Carver grunts against it, sighs as the idol slides out. Red droplets dot its silver tip. He's pressed harder than Reza last night, but she can't tell what effect that might have.

A warm realization fills her chest. She's been too

horrified by her own bodily surprises today to think of the idol's greater applications. How Carver might feel. What he might need to patch a hole in his heart.

What glories the severed horn off a god's penis could grant a man like him.

⚧

Deep in the night, Carver stirs beside Reza on the couch. They turned off the lights and have been watching television, drifting off, waking, too excited for true sleep. The pressure keeps aching between Reza's thighs, but she doesn't know how to help that, or herself.

She can only help Carver as the miracle punches new flesh from his body.

He trembles in her arms as power twists at his groin. Strange sensations must now be reaching, reaching, grasping at the world, except he isn't surrounded by strangers in a waiting room. He's with Reza, and she loves him, and she wants him to feel alive and whole, whatever that means for him.

The blanket slides from his body as his silhouette stands shakily against the flickering television light. It reflects off relieved tears and offers a dark glimpse of much-desired change standing below Carver's waist.

A blessing granted by a god.

Carver turns to Reza in cautious inches. He catches her staring, wondering, the television light flickering over all the interests he's set down—the guitar, the paintings, the love of his life.

And he must feel the longing pressure between his thighs, same as Reza feels it, curse of a god's touch, a clitoral itch she can no longer scratch. She sits up to ask if he's okay, if there's anything she can do.

His shadow lowers across her, and every possible word melts in the heat of his deepest kiss. His hands push up her top and paw at her sweatpants. Her hands find his goatee, his chest, his scars, the new flesh stretching and hardening below, and her fingers lock around the shaft. He reaches past her and then slides cool fluid over his member the way he used to turn a strap-on slippery, only now it's him, his body, nothing else.

"Carver," Reza whispers between kisses. "I don't—I can't open like that anymore."

But she's already naked beneath his touch. He can see and feel the difference on her, and his fingers share slickness across her changed anatomy. She gasps without meaning to as that unending pressure both swells and sighs. Has this been what her transformation has wanted all along? A tender hand?

Carver pauses, waiting for Reza to slide away, leave him. She instead grasps his face again for another kiss, and another, and then draws him atop her. The pressure aches, but that's fine; Carver must be feeling the same. The price of magic in them, side effects of a god. Reza lets the worry slip away as hers and Carver's members slide against each other, against their thighs, their muscles tensing together in a storm of kisses and grasping, and then the eternal pressure bursts in unexpected sweetness, the ease of twin universes born wet and warm between lovers.

They tremble heavily into the couch cushions, clutching and laughing. Reza cradles Carver's head. She couldn't have imagined enjoying this before. Enjoying him, always, but her change? Never, or so she thought. But it has only been a day, and maybe she needs to give it time. Some are born with this flesh, and some without, and there are all kinds of complicated details you can learn about bodies and desires and what you want of yourself.

Maybe genuine magic has offered a gift Reza desires after all. At least with Carver.

At least for tonight.

The world is still dark outside when the picture window shatters inward. Glass rains through the living room, and the calamity wakes Reza and Carver in a tangled panic. Their limbs have twisted together in sleep, and they now form a writhing mess as a figure climbs over broken-glass teeth, past the sill, into their house.

Television light flickers across Charlotte's red hair. Her grimace. Her steel baseball bat.

How long did she follow Reza yesterday? She couldn't have tried her hit-and-run at the yard sale site by happenstance. No, she must have followed from clinic, to house, away to yard sale site, but now she's back, and she's waited until deep in the night to catch Reza and Carver off-guard.

And to do worse.

"Run," Reza whispers, pulling a leg from under Carver. "Run, babe, please, run."

Carver staggers to his feet as Charlotte charges. She smashes the bat against the small of his back, and he tumbles against the couch, crying out. Charlotte doesn't watch him, doesn't care. She only gives another whack to keep him from protecting her true prey.

The bat aims at Reza. "If it wasn't for a thing like you, I'd still have my life!" Charlotte cries. She pinwheels the bat at one side, has been practicing the move for a night of breaking bones and spilling blood.

Steel crashes across Reza's shoulder. She drops onto the glass-strewn carpet, each fragment biting her arms, breasts, belly. Her hands splay to grab a weapon, maybe a window shard, a sneaker, anything.

Her fingers grope at knotted wood.

Charlotte howls, charging again. "If it wasn't for a thing like you, he wouldn't have left me!"

Reza doesn't know who Charlotte means, or why she has murder in her eyes. If they could sit to talk things over, maybe Reza could know why Charlotte so badly hates a woman with a dick, someone she doesn't even know.

There's no talking it out with murder, no understanding. Reza can only grasp the one object in reach, thick as her forearm, and try to put a stop to this.

Both hands seize the idol, and Reza drives its silver tip into Charlotte's gut.

Charlotte raises the bat again and slams Reza's head, but Reza has to press on through the sudden white spots, the screaming pain. She reels back and drives the idol's tip into Charlotte's flesh again, this time her underbelly, and then her thigh, and then her bicep, shoulder, chest. The last of these blows knocks Charlotte to the carpet, but it isn't the final blow. Reza keeps stabbing silver into muscle and skin, again and again.

Blood streaks the idol's tip and splatters its knobby shaft. Faster now, blood coating wood, its own lubricant, greasing this godly phallus as if gearing for orgasm.

Quickening the magic.

Charlotte screams as a pale penis erupts from her belly, through Reza's first stab wound. Another juts inches below, eating flesh from the first. A third member splashes bloody from Charlotte's thigh, and then from her arm, shoulder, chest, and more.

Each growth feeds from its surroundings. Some glimmer with flecks of bone. Others weave hair with skin. A few come wreathed in living room carpet fibers, bits of Charlotte's clothing, traces of steel from her baseball bat.

Reza keeps stabbing, and the newest flesh sucks at her knees. She doesn't care. She drives the idol's silver top into Charlotte's waist, her face, her eye socket. Her blows only stop when Carver hauls her back.

But he can't stop what she's started.

Muscles unthread, bones fragment, organs disperse. Charlotte writhes as every part of her core drains into a twisting mass of phallus upon phallus, as if that is all she has been and all she can be, from beginning to end. Her throbbing form swells through every shaft and tip, sucking at floor, wallpaper, even taking on the myriad colors of Carver's dusty paintings.

Reza is almost too shaken to notice the scarlet-robed figures climbing through her broken picture window.

"O gift of blood, we taste him again!" one shouts.

"Beloved stranger with strange magics," says another, the tallest of them.

They make no motion to approach Reza and Carver, instead descending on the writhing phallic mass in a dance of scarlet and shadow. Robes climb thighs as the figures lower themselves onto the thing that used to be Charlotte. Their numbers swell in uncertain genders, but each flashes a hungry vulva, and each of those finds stiff flesh to devour.

Carver clutches Reza tight, and she lets him. She's done fighting.

The people of the scarlet-robed throng hold hands while their bodies work against flesh, and their conjoined orgasmic scream ripples down the phallus-coated monstrosity. This cry is joyous yet ear-splitting, calling an unearthly name beyond letters, beyond speech.

Beneath them, the calmed abomination slips wetly from between their thighs, member by member, and each damp tower of flesh retracts into the rising body like a sheathed cat claw. The once-Charlotte flesh stretches through the broken window, forming enormous legs stepping out of the living room and onto the lawn. One, two, learning to grow and walk outside the house as a fledgling giant.

Or maybe a god.

The scarlet-robed throng clambers to follow.

"Wait," Reza says, prying herself from Carver's grasp. She lowers her head in reverence and holds out the silver-tipped idol. "He'll need this, won't he?"

The living room bustles with escaping bodies as strong hands lift the weight from Reza's fingers. She glances up in time to see the tallest scarlet-robed figure smile at her, and then the throng slips as one through the broken picture window.

Reza follows to the sill, Carver behind her.

Silhouettes dart beneath a purple-black sky, pregnant with eventual sunrise. One figure heads off the enormous fleshy legs, the torso, arms, and head still forming from the waist. The scarlet-robed figure raises the idol toward the titan, and his gargantuan steps slow. One enormous hand grasps the idol, the half-made head nods gratitude, and then the titan fixes the idol between his legs.

Only as the sky reddens and the figures turn to vanish with the night does Reza glimpse the shadow swinging between the tremendous legs, a divine member, at last regaining its silver-tipped horn.

An incarnate god, alive and whole.

A SCREAM LIGHTS UP THE SKY

JOE KOCH

THEY'RE NAKED UNDER the sun, sprawled on the sand with too many arms. Still human, their bellies swell with the things, blistering from sunburn, bruising from inside. Bubbles form on crimson-purple skin. Boils glow white with fluid pressure, stretched over enlarged abdomens. The big round globes rotate above extra appendages that sprout black and hairy from their ribs and hips. Extra legs elongate in the last moments before birthing starts.

Kaiden whispers to Charlie, "Shit, they're close. If we—"

Charlie bolts up to make a run for the lighthouse. Kaiden grabs the loose strap on their backpack and yanks them back behind the little upside-down rowboat. "Keep down. They're about to hatch."

Kaiden ignores the flash of hurt across Charlie's face as they land with a muffled thunk on the sand. Jaw jutting out, their dark eyes pout. Charlie doesn't need to say a word to remind Kaiden this is all their damn fault. It was Kaiden's idea to flee the city for some vaguely remembered vacation spot. They should know by now there's no refuge, nowhere to run.

Necks wag. Mouths drool. It's hard for Kaiden to believe the breeders are human; better to forget if you want to sleep at night. The mutating torsos writhe. Pulsing white blisters on their bellies gawk and roil at Kaiden like a predatory chorus of glowing spider eyes.

Charlie shifts up, poised in a low crouch, eyes glued on the mutated wombs about to burst with new life. "No way. I'm not waiting here to get swarmed."

Kaiden grabs the wooden underside of the little rowboat and says, "If we can get underneath this thing and dig in. Help me."

Kaiden lifts. Charlie stands and shoves the boat down. "Are you crazy? Come on!"

Knuckles mashed, Kaiden gasps with shock. Charlie takes off across the sand. Hitting patches of sea oats, they struggle to find footing, sliding in the high dunes. Charlie seems to run in slow motion, stuck in place fifteen feet away from Kaiden with the shelter of the keeper's cabin and the lighthouse far from reach.

Sunburned skin tears open on the breeders' overgrown torsos. Blisters pop. Milky fluid oozes down, dribbling over deflated breasts and upside-down chins. Wallowing on their backs, with new and old appendages evenly splayed on each side, the breeders raise their swollen bellies up off the sand, arching their backs on all eight limbs.

Heads droop in delirium. The brand-new limbs at the ribs and hips bristle with what looks like thick hair. It's really an excess of networked cilia that function as nipples to feed their young, although births are so numerous the entire limb is typically devoured. The hairy look makes Kaiden's mind race back to lying to their ex about PCOS before they came out. Kaiden should make a decision to either run and help Charlie or hide under the boat, but guilt clogs their response and reminds them how their ex lectured them on fertility, on the health benefits of breastfeeding, on the risks of surgeries Kaiden hadn't even begun to contemplate when they finally confided. Maybe honesty was a mistake, or maybe the relationship failed due to Kaiden's delay. Either way, Kaiden's angry that the guilt still plagues them, angry at their ex for reducing them mentally to nothing but a set of organs, and angry at Charlie for running and leaving them alone with yet another choice that gets harder to make the longer they wait.

Spider-walking breeders span the shoreline. Tiny wagging heads turn towards the beach where Charlie slides in the sand. Faces split into yawning gapes. The slopped-out milky fluid from broken blisters clings to cheeks, chins, and lips. Heaving up young with a guttural hawking sound that reverberates in a vomitous sonata, they give birth from their throats. Newborn creatures scurry out shiny, many-legged, and cockroach-brown in color, cutting the distended edges of lips smeared with maternal blood and the spilled white slime.

Wormy and amorphous beneath shards of chitinous shell, nothing earthly or comprehensible, squirming machines engineered from fecal waste, the newborns hungrily chew at the hairy auxiliary limbs of their mothers. Quickly nourished and ready to mate, they cavort across the dunes towards Charlie with reproductive suckers erect.

Kaiden seizes an oar as a weapon. The spawned creatures spin fast as starfish across the dunes. White dervish clouds of sand billow from the onslaught. Kaiden dives forward in Charlie's direction, scrambling through the sandstorm into the line of attack.

The sand is blinding and stings Kaiden's skin. In contrast, the wet clinging warmth of the creatures comforts and seduces as they release hormones that penetrate Kaiden's pores. Familiar images mingle with disgust, flooding Kaiden's mind with a sudden sense of false and sickening nostalgia. Hopes they never had tug at their heart. The poison twists their memory into an old photograph that never existed.

Kaiden and Charlie are on the porch of a white farmhouse in the picture, arm in arm. Kaiden has seen houses like this in their dreams for years. They have a weird deja-vu whenever they pass one on a rural highway.

Such farmhouses are a common sight, set back between fields and silos, houses made for big families and optimistic futures leftover from an idyllic era before Kaiden was born. They hold the idea of a home, imprinted on Kaiden's deepest desire for belonging, stability, and continuity; the idea of home as a bigger self to dwell in. The white farmhouse haunts Kaiden's unconscious hopes.

The happy couple stands arm in arm on the porch, smiling for the camera until an intrusive thought disrupts Kaiden's romance. The voice is a warning: *No one will save this picture in an album. No one will remain. Your history ends here because you never had children. Your love will die, forgotten.*

Kaiden quits fighting off the warm dark things that nurse at their skin with the texture of slugs. Maybe they share a mutual need. After all, it hurts to deny the want of the awful hungry things; hurts to turn away from their longing, leave them unfulfilled, and break the bond of contact. Will not love sprung from one's body surpass all other loves? The Self can die and something else lives on. Kaiden can become part of a greater whole.

Soft bodies explore Kaiden's skin, seeking mucus membranes to impregnate. Biological traits don't matter; all humans have vulnerable tissues the breeders can convert to their purpose. In Kaiden's vision, the photograph of the white farmhouse fragments into sections like a kaleidoscope: the world seen through the eyes of an insect. Then the sections dissolve and Kaiden is underwater, blinded by chlorine stinging their eyes. But it isn't chlorine in the water; it's sand, and Kaiden isn't underwater. This is the middle of a fight.

The sticky, needy things nursing along their neck and nudging into their shorts with invasive branching reproductive suckers are monsters. And they will turn Kaiden into a monster.

Kaiden digs in anger underneath exoskeletons and squeezes fast and hard. Pus squirts out from under the shells. They yank the wriggling things off and stomp them into the sand. They'll worry about prying the ends of the suckers out later. Trails of sticky branches hang from their arms and jaw. The fuckers got close to winning. Kaiden hoists the oar like a baseball bat over their shoulder and swings at the thick swarm.

"Fuck you!" They swing again. And again, harder. "Fuck you, you stupid fuckers!"

Because that's all they are. Fuckers. Things that gestate in a few hours, feast on their host, and die the minute they shoot their load. No mind, no soul. They create nothing, think nothing, and love nothing. Kaiden hates them. Rage builds with each blow. The slam and crunch of impact fuels Kaiden's laughter and satisfaction. A violent wave of triumph keeps them swinging long after the bulk of the swarm drops.

In the settled sandstorm, Kaiden halts. A few feet away, the bottom of a shoe, a ball cap tumbling on the breeze, and in between a lumpy, moving mass that fills Kaiden with despair. Under attack Charlie is a pulsing horde of brownish-red impossibilities, of many-legged incongruent underbellies, a waste dump of fecal-tinged tentacle shapes and spurting organs feeding and fucking with multipurpose mouths.

Kaiden aims, slamming the oar down on the middle of the swarm. Fingers crossed they'll crack more shells than ribs. Bruised balls are a fair price for birth control. Kaiden clears the creatures, more worried about the mucous membranes accessible on Charlie's face than those clinging to their clothes. They drop the oar. They sink to their knees slathered in pinkish-brown goo. Through a chitinous splatter of broken shells, they pluck the wormy yet crab-like yet plant-structured things from Charlie's neck, ripping away infant creatures one by one. Kaiden shakes off guilty messages prodding their conscience.

There's no way the things could be making human sounds when they have the mouthparts of a starfish or anemone. Kaiden crushes the creatures before they latch and mate, trying to ignore the high-pitched cries. So what if their squeals of distress sound the same as a healthy human baby. *It's only noise*, Kaiden thinks.

It doesn't mean anything.

Kaiden pries another from Charlie's chin. Charlie's lips are clamped tight. Kaiden can almost breathe again. Nothing got in.

It's okay. We're okay.

Two more to go. One peeled from Charlie's cheek reveals a glassy, intoxicated, unpenetrated eye. Kaiden grasps the last. It doesn't squirm. It doesn't cry.

The entire eye is covered, obscured by the suckering branches of an erection that meet to form a tube, a tiny tree folded like a Japanese fan. The shell is intact and the body hangs flaccid and dead. When Kaiden pulls the sticky mating tube, tentacled lips hold tight around the socket.

Prying from the outer corner, Kaiden's careful not to pop out Charlie's eyeball. Maybe they kept it closed all this time. Maybe the translucent gobbets of fluid leaking out as Kaiden works the tube of branches loose didn't make contact with the delicate tissues underneath Charlie's eyelid or the soft pink tear duct near the bridge of their nose.

The fluid coating is so thick it mimics an eyelid. Kaiden's heart jumps with hope.

Then the liquid sluices away like pearlescent tears. Charlie's eye shines wide open with conjunctival mucous membranes exposed.

"No," Kaiden says. "This is all my fault. I'm so sorry."

Charlie smiles up at Kaiden, waking happily, dosed with endorphins and hormones. Spreading their arms ecstatic, Charlie stretches as if the piles of mashed remains on the sand were a luxurious featherbed. "Hey, babe." They shift closer to Kaiden. Their voice is cloying and seductive. "None of that self-hatred kink allowed today. We can find a better way to make you come."

Kaiden swallows their disgust at the smell of the freshly killed creatures baking in the heat of the sun. "I just thought—I remembered this place from when I was a kid. My brother and his girlfriend brought me with them. It seemed so romantic here. And after what happened with you and Kelsey—but we both saw it coming, even before that. It wasn't like I thought we'd be one hundred percent safe here, but maybe safer than the city. Mostly I thought it would help fix things between us."

"Then what are you doing way over there?"

"I'm trying to explain to you and apologize because I know you think I'm just stupid half the time and I know you're going to hate me for what I have to do. I'll try to make it easy on you."

"I love you," Charlie says, too warmly. It's not like them to be maudlin or miss a chance to evaluate Kaiden's flaws. They didn't even get mad at Kaiden for bringing up Kelsey again. "Come here and kiss me so I can show you how much."

Kaiden runs through a quick mental inventory of the necessary supplies. "I think I brought everything we need to take care of your problem. Fucking infuriating timetable." They scoot closer despite the rank odor of the murdered horde rising from Charlie's clothes and skin. Why not? They're covered in filth, too. Untangling bits of shattered shells from Charlie's long hair, eyeing the breeders by the shore, some surviving, some dead, Kaiden says, "Let's get you cleaned up and out of the sun before we start your abortion, okay?"

Tides wash away the sand beneath the dead breeders, tugging them toward deeper waters. The ocean claims the bodies, inch by inch. A gelatinous noise bubbles up from the living. Bags of skin shrivel on their bones; depleted flesh heaves together, hugging and sobbing in sickening euphoria. Postpartum sweat glistens and streams from broken skin. Afterbirth drools from cracked lips leaving long sticky threads. Mouths are torn, blistered, and inflamed at the corners. Through fitful giggling and tears, they coagulate in a fleshy puddle. Visceral ejaculations replace human speech. Rocking and wailing in a feral heap, the agglutinated sirens discharge music that calls all within aural range to participate in their shared uterine bond.

Kaiden's hypnotized by the horror of the sound. The alien desire fills them with dread. They rip their eyes away from the bizarre ritual on the shore and turn to tend to Charlie's dangerous condition.

Charlie leaps on top of Kaiden. Kaiden tumbles backwards in surprise. Charlie shoves their tongue in Kaiden's mouth. Kaiden twists their head away. Charlie's neck snakes in synchronicity, kissing Kaiden with relentless passion. Kaiden tries to cry out as Charlie gets hard against them. Maybe this isn't a good time. Their voice is crammed full of Charlie's mouth. Soft and snaking tongue tasting of familiar raw sweetness and in a flash Kaiden forgets everything except the thrill of pleasure and connection with their lover's touch. It's been so long between the drama with Kelsey and the spread of the breeders and now for a few seconds there is nothing else in the universe except this: no repulsion, no regret, no guilt.

Nothing else matters. It's difficult to breathe, but holding contact feels too good to stop. Arms on either side of Kaiden strain to support the new weight. Already growing, expanding, evolving, Charlie's torso hangs low. The fat abdomen grazes Kaiden's diaphragm. Plump mounds rise on Charlie's lean pecs. Kaiden can't resist testing one between a forefinger and thumb. Charlie gasps at the pressure of a light pinch.

Charlie knees Kaiden's thighs farther apart. Kaiden bites Charlie's neck. Charlie moans and fumbles, unable to maneuver around their sudden overgrown belly. Kaiden reaches down and guides them inside, lifts their own hips, and holds the swelling abdomen higher with both hands so Charlie can thrust. The sensation of their lover's body changing, morphing, growing in their grasp fascinates Kaiden with terror as the sound of the sirens breeds a lullaby of fucking. Passionate as sleepwalking succubae, heaving and shaken apart with screams of lust in a mind-core that must be shared psychosis or cosmic union, Kaiden sees the squirming reddish-brown embryos rushing to maturity under Charlie's skin. The taste of them on Charlie's lips and neck is a circle of infinite insect fulfillment, the trembling of shattered flesh inside a million tiny mirrors screaming *life, life, life*. Life for the sake of proliferation and colonization; life untethered by doubt, self-reflection, or the lugubrious weight of philosophical chains. Life that crawls, swims, flies, fucks, and makes more life at all costs, through all bodies, and in all worlds. Fucking toward explosive redundancy as the sirens on the beach chant *hatch, hatch, hatch,* Charlie and Kaiden burn through the gestational period in seizures of directionless heat and collapse in a vast orgasm of manic laughter.

Coming down in a blackout, Kaiden catches a vision of the white farmhouse again. Instead of sadness at the sight of the photo that will be lost with no legacy rooting it in the future, Kaiden elates at the multiplicity of similar relics bound in the album. The snapshot is one of many collected in family albums over generations. Countless accumulate, memorializing their love. It fills Kaiden with pride: there they stand on the porch, Charlie and Kaiden, smiles on their faces, arms encircling one another's waists. Except Charlie doesn't look quite the same as Kaiden remembers. Something isn't quite right.

Kaiden flips through the other pictures trying to figure out what's different. It might be a blur across Charlie's features or shadows that fall a bit wrong. Kaiden can't put their finger on what unsettles them. Nausea pokes at their stomach. The hint of a gag reflex tickles the back of their throat.

Cockroach-brown grease is smeared across the plastic sleeves. Looking closer, the thing on the porch with Kaiden is badly out of focus in almost every picture. Where Charlie should smile, shaky little mimics gather: piles of shells and legs. An assembly of small slimy creatures with too many legs imitating Charlie's face, hands, shins; page after page, they squirm beneath Kaiden's fingers. They come to life and writhe up from the slits in the plastic sleeves.

Kaiden flings down the album and stomps. Soft bodies squirt across the floor. Shells crack. Layers of brown goo turn the room into a pond. Kaiden retches at the hot dead stench and slips on the sludge. They fall rolling on the floor, rolling in the sand, not laughing with their lover anymore but sobbing beside them on the beach by the lighthouse; rolling, scratching, beating the image of the invasive creatures off of their body as they wake from a bad dream.

From bad dream into worse reality, Kaiden wakes to realize hours have passed.

"I love you," Kaiden says, uncertain if Charlie can understand language. Their flesh feels hot. Residue comes away at Kaiden's touch.

Languishing in the muck-brown filth as sunset casts long pink shadows across the sand, Charlie twists their limbs as if some invisible giant molds them, shaping and coiling their arms into useless abominations. Bits cling to Kaiden's fingers and palms like melted plastic. Curious, Kaiden licks. The taste is too floral, like ingesting the scent of peonies in bloom.

Kaiden spits.

Soft insistent growths mangle Charlie's clothes. New knobs of extra limbs sprout from their ribs and hips pushing through fabric already strained by the bulbous globe of abdomen that stretches toward the sky. With similar tropism, the breeders stretch out over the dunes and circle in closer, dragging their mass like roiling starfish across the sand. Continuing the sickening hymn of their siren song, they circle Kaiden and Charlie like a garland of meaty flowers with rooting appendages intertwined. The breeders drone and wail. Charlie's features blur into an uncertain lumpy contradiction. A liquid noise bubbles from their throat and blends with the sound of the sirens as Charlie gurgles out imitative song.

Pink, tar-like discharge drips from their mouth. Kaiden catches words like *beautiful*, *excited*, *family*, and *forever*. Every physical sign says it's almost too late for an abortion. "Calm down," Kaiden says, unbuttoning Charlie's cargo shorts. "Keep still."

Overly sweet, the sloughed off flesh sickens with its cloying scent. Kaiden cleans their hands with gritty sand and pulls gloves out of the backpack. "I'm sorry," they say, even though it's useless to expect Charlie to listen now—not that they were ever a good listener. Kaiden still can't resist the compulsion to explain and apologize. "I hope you're too wacked out to feel this. I'm doing my best, okay? I've never done this before. I promise I'll try to make it quick."

Kaiden pulls off Charlie's cargo shorts exposing the remnant of a cock. The shifting rose-shaped organ looks bloodless with its surface of wrinkled gray skin, but as Kaiden peels back the petal-like layers of the pseudo-flower, reddish membranes pulse, lively within. The sticky flesh seeks to re-knit at every flayed stretch. Kaiden fishes for duct tape in the backpack and uses it to clamp down the peeled-away flaps, gradually teasing the tiny aperture into an adequately sized vagina.

Charlie wails with each peeled-back strip of penile flesh. Keeping time with the circling sirens, an upswing ends the cadence of their every gasp. Charlie groans something sensuous that sounds like, *God, yes*. Kaiden flushes with embarrassment and slaps duct tape on the last loose flap.

Dad would be proud, Kaiden thinks at the sight of the duct-taped vulvar construction. Their whole house seemed held together by duct tape growing up. It turned into a running joke as the kids grew older. When problems hit, they'd use "Dad voice" and say "*Well kiddo, you know there's one way to fix that*" and offer ridiculous suggestions. Even later, with divorce, addiction, and jail time, it was shorthand for saying things would be okay when they would never be the same. The last time Kaiden's brother cried on their shoulder once the breeders had begun to spread, all they had to do was hug him and whisper "*Duct tape, bro*."

In Dad voice, Kaiden says out loud, "This is no time for jokes, kiddo."

They snort out a little laugh, because it is time; because the opening below Charlie's urethra unfolds like an empty eye socket shedding a single tear of healthy, red, human-colored blood. Charlie pants with erotic abandon, an unpleasant side effect Kaiden didn't expect to witness. The vulvar opening blinks and pulsates in rhythm with Charlie's sensuous aroused movements. *Oh yes*, Kaiden thinks. *Shit is fucked up. It is definitely time for jokes.*

Kaiden presses the tips of all five fingers of their right hand together and pushes them into the undulating eye. Charlie twitches and moans. The circle of breeders around the pair coils in closer as the muscles inside Charlie's body tighten around Kaiden's wrist.

Think of an animal. Think of a cow.

Kaiden shoves hard. Their hand breaks a barrier. Charlie groans. Sunk in up to the elbow, Kaiden would cry if it weren't so funny, so goddamn funny.

Like a cow. On a farm. We'll laugh about this later.

(If Charlie survives.)

Kaiden feels for embryos. The tears blurring their eyes don't matter since they have to search by hand. They grasp a thick fatty appendage inside a slick membrane. A knob of sorts on the end, thick enough to tether between two fingers. Kaiden clamps their fist and yanks it out.

Pink sky turns red with sunset's end. The writhing roots of the circling sirens dance like strange fire climbing up to touch the rising moon, moved by a new lunar tropism. The shining wet placenta slops out onto the sand in a steaming mass. Liquid pours from Charlie's orifice. Shrieks gush from Charlie's throat. Kaiden throws the sac aside and rips off the duct tape. They close the wound, pressing the sticky shreds together. The result is more like raw hamburger than rosebud or human cock, but at least Kaiden's efforts stop the bleeding.

A sour smell of lilac and rotten milk rises in the red evening light. Kaiden rips off the gloves and rubs away the last of the tears trembling on their lashes. The unruptured placenta holds only one creature inside. Curled like a comma and pearly as a nautilus shell, it's plump and shiny with Charlie's bodily fluid. The head is round, pinkish, and tilted down. Two tiny fists clench and unclench. Two feet kick at the suffocating barrier of the liquid-filled sac. Kaiden thinks of billboards saying a baby has a heartbeat at six weeks.

But this isn't six weeks, not even six hours. This isn't a baby. This can't be human no matter what it looks like.

"I'm hallucinating," Kaiden says out loud.

No one is listening. Charlie metamorphoses beside them in a pile of metabolic processes Kaiden can't understand. The vining fire of the entwined sirens circles like a strange wreathe, mutating into flaming shadows under the crimson-stained moonlight; a fleshy ocean forest closing in to claim their precious young.

Alone in the center of the fire that is not a fire, Kaiden grabs the placental sac and bursts through the writhing ring of sirens in a wild leap. Past the keeper's cabin, Kaiden pummels the sand and runs. The wind on the night-beach bites colder. Up the small, steep steps, they hug the wall as a storm sweeps in from the gleaming black horizon. Round and round against the unsettling incline of the tower and out through the last rattling door to the balcony, Kaiden clutches the creature all the way to the top of the lighthouse.

It squirms against their chest with human need.

A SCREAM LIGHTS UP THE SKY

Winded from the climb, Kaiden wonders what animates the small body without it taking a breath. Sealed inside the membrane, the thing should be drowned. Yet the heft of it settling into the crook of Kaiden's arm and the soft hungry way it gropes at their scars suggests the impossible made manifest.

The sea storm roars. Riotous waves slap the rocks below. Screaming winds from the ocean drown out any apology whispered through Kaiden's salt-sore throat.

The floor of the balcony leans out and down towards the sea. Kaiden pitches forward, leaning hips into the hard railing. They hold the squirming, struggling thing upside-down by one foot. They hold it out over the ledge with one hand and use the other to open the placenta.

Fluid pours out in many colors. The storm lights up the sky. Winged insects or cherubs dive in and out of the sea, churning the waves to rise. Foam sprays against the balcony. Water seeks water. Flesh seeks entropy. Eyes of fire collide. Kaiden's shoulder strains as the thing attached to the foot twists, beating at the chaotic air. Its mouth opens. It takes its first breath. The liquid release of the slick membrane of placenta now pierced, the night sky is torn asunder. The ruptured firmament shrieks with echoes of many mind-shattering cries. In answer to the brute symphony of the storm, all Kaiden can do is scream.

LONG FINGERS

LAYNE VAN RENSBURG

THERE IS A finger in my morning coffee. The digit, a repetition of middle and proximal phalanges, originates behind the bread bin and seems quite pleased to be scalding its pale flesh in my expresso. At first, I think it is a snake, a worm, or a wire. Something that makes sense.

I scream. There isn't much emotion behind it. It just feels like something I *have* to do, you know? A ritual that needs to be completed. An acknowledgement of the fact there is an impossible finger in my brew.

When I am done screaming, I grab a steak knife. I haven't even used it before—it was a wedding present, from a friend who didn't know I had just become vegan. I hesitate. It might be easiest if I cut it off at the proximal interphalangeal joint, plaster the hole, and never think about this again. The whole situation is weird enough that I'll eventually remember it as a dream.

It would be such a hassle to clean that up. No, I'll take a more reasoned approach.

Knife ready, hands glistening in nervous sweat, I move the bread bin out of the way to better see where the finger comes from. The hole had apparently been made from inside the wall—debris lines the counter just outside of it. It is just a bit bigger than the finger and I can see where it joins to the hand.

What shape is this thing that is living in my wall? This isn't America, where the walls are large enough for a person to uncomfortably squeeze into—there is no way that thing is remotely human. How long had it been there? Did it grow there like a fungus, or migrate from somewhere else? How is it sustaining itself?

These questions spin around my head for minutes before I decide to do something very stupid. I gently place my knife beneath the sixth and seventh joints of finger, I lift it out of the coffee. Brown liquid drips from its blistered red skin onto the marble counter. I lay it down by the bread bin and take my cup away, out of reach.

I sip the coffee. Still hot.

"Ouch," I say, staring at the painful red topography at the end of the digit. The poor thing probably didn't mean to scald itself like that. I get a jug, fill it part way with cool water, and just a bit of ice from the freezer, then leave it by the hole. After a delay, the finger wiggles its way clumsily into the glass. It is warm inside the house, so no risk of hypothermia.

I retrieve the first aid kit and set about disinfecting the finger. It is pliable in my hands, unagitated by my contact with its sensitive skin.

"Thanks," a voice says from the sink.

"No problem," I tell it. I throw on my jacket and grab my bag. I am going to miss the bus at this rate.

On the bus to work, I text Will: "Hey babe, hope the conference is going well. Maybe stay out of town. We've got pests. I'll be getting a hotel after work." It doesn't seem like the time to go into detail about the nature of the pests. Will doesn't need to be stressed about this yet. Before the bus stops, I notice a bit of skin stuck between my teeth and pick it out when no one is looking. It's from the finger. I place it carefully in some cling film that I tear off my wrapped lunch.

St. Joan's Clinic welcomes me with tired-eyed patients and staff, and a sterile scent that reminds me where I am. I realise I forgot to brush my hair. But that's not unusual, so no one comments on it. With another cup of coffee in hand, I check on the intakes from last night.

A man with severe alcohol poisoning bit the end of his tongue off. "My hea' hurs," he mumbles. I give him a smile and remind him to drink plenty of fluid. There's a large bottle of water next to his bed, hardly touched.

I barely have time to drink my coffee before someone comes in with their middle finger bent back almost ninety degrees. I let Carly handle him.

It's not a busy day, relatively speaking, but it keeps my mind off things. At least until my break. My corner—Jennifer's Corner, as my colleagues say—is waiting for me. For once, I'd actually like people to bother me about workplace gossip but it's too much to expect. I can hear them talking about how Carly hooked up with a twenty-year-old—again.

"Hey guys," I whisper. "How's your morning been? Oh mine? Well, my house is being invaded by an impossible organism."

They'd think I finally lost it.

With my curiosity growing, I quickly finish my lunch, and take off to the labs. I have enough purpose in my step and tension in my shoulders that the technicians don't question my presence. To make sure they really have no reason to bother me I don a pair of latex gloves before I take out the bit of cling film with a flake of epidermis in it. I place that under the microscope and zoom in as far as I can, 400x.

I see the rigid structure I'm expecting—an impenetrable wall of dead keratinocytes. Except . . . they're not dead. Processes extend out of their nuclei, crossing out of and into cell walls, forming a kind of network. There are other cell types too. A few macrophages, I think, except they're much faster than I expect macrophages to be, and they're dividing. They shouldn't be dividing—presumably these are pro-inflammatory macrophages. Their purpose is to eat whatever threatens the exposed body and then die. They're terminally differentiated, incapable of division in this environment.

I pocket the sample again.

Will has texted me back by the time I'm home. "What pests? Are you okay? Call me." He's sweet. Still outside the house, I FaceTime him.

"You okay, babe?" he asks. "You look like a draugr." I smile. I got him into *Skyrim* a few weeks ago. He's already put more hours in than I have. Easier to do when you always have your laptop with you.

"Yeah. Listen . . . I'm not sure how to tell you this. I'll just show you." I enter the kitchen and point the camera at the hole the finger came out of. It's retreated now.

"Whoa, how did that happen?" he asks.

"Something dug its way out from the inside. Hang on." I turn on the hot water tap and fill a mug. I add some coffee. It is warm but not scalding like before. I leave it beside the hole and set my phone up, so it has a good view inside.

"What's going on?" Will asks.

"Again, you're not going to believe me, so I need to just show you." If it weren't for the skin in my bag, I might have believed I imagined the whole thing. That the stress of work had gotten to me. But I saw it. And now it squirms its way out of the hole again.

"Is that a snake? Get away from it!" I don't say anything, just release the breath I've been holding. He can see it. I let him watch it for a moment as it dips itself in the coffee. "Wait, it's all bony. It's . . . a finger? What the hell, babe?"

"Yeah, I don't know what it is, or how it got here. But

it's harmless so far." It's no longer burnt—at all. Either it's a different finger or it can heal much faster than we can.

"I think you should get out of the house," Will says. "It's not safe. You can come to my hotel."

"It is safe," I tell him. I touch the finger. Will screams for me to stop. He goes quiet when my hand is gently curled around it, and he realizes it does him no good. "I'm going to try to figure out what I can about it. Talk later. Love you." I end the call.

The hand is still there—I lift it out of the impromptu coffee and inspect its tip. Little pores open and close along the side, like it's breathing. At least its behaviour makes more sense. To confirm that it reacts to heat, I fill up a glass with plain, hot water and take away the coffee. It enters the glass. The water level slowly decreases.

The sink. I remember it speaking before I left. With a torch in hand, I shine a light down it. It's difficult to make out but there's something hard and reflective lining the pipe. Teeth, surrounded by a matrix of organic matter, food, and flesh.

"What are you?" I ask.

"What are you?" it echoes in a distant voice. The true mouth, the one capable of speech with a larynx, must be further down.

"I'm Jennifer. This is my home."

"Jennifer. Home," it says back. Either it really does have only rudimentary intelligence, or it's messing with me.

"I'll pour bleach down on you," I tell it.

"Bleach bleach."

"It will hurt," I say.

It goes quiet. Then sobs. It sounds like a little girl. "No hurt, no hurt," it gets out between choking back tears. "Sorrysorrysorry," it says. I can hear the phlegm.

"There there, I won't hurt you. *I'm* sorry," I say.

The crying takes a while to die down completely. "Thank you," it says again. "Water? Water please?"

I let the cool water run down the drain. It's quiet for a while. "Thank you."

"No problem, whatever you are." I fill a plastic bucket with water and wash my dishes outside.

The next day at work, I mingle for once. Everyone has congregated to the central sofa of the break room, so I sit on the separate seat facing them. They're quiet at first. Eventually Richard asks, "Did you hear about the teratoma they found in the lab general waste bin?"

I shake my head. "No. How did it get there?"

"That's the thing," Carly adds. "No one knows. There are no records of any recent surgeries. It's baffling. Oh, and they found it inside a glove. Creepy."

"Maybe it grew there," Richard jokes. Ann laughs.

"What's happened to it now?"

Richard yawns. "I think it's been moved to the correct bin. I guess there should be an investigation, but no one really wants to deal with that. What, are you okay?"

The tears come without my knowledge. I leave without answering Richard, head to the lab, and then towards the nearest waste room. The colour-coded bins line the walls. Purple (cytotoxic), yellow (highly infectious), orange (infectious) and finally red (anatomical). It's the kind of bin you don't want to open unless necessary.

But before I can persuade myself not to, I'm fumbling with latches.

I cover my nose. Beneath me, a red stew of placentas, wound dressings, and bowel tissue. It smells worse than anything. *This is people,* I think. I scan the bin, frantically looking for something remotely like a teratoma—and there, clinging to the corner, is a swirl of brown hair, matted with blood. I hesitate. What am I even doing?

The thing leaps at me, and I fall. It leaves a trail of viscera as it paces back and forth over my chest with its fat little legs. With a sigh, I lean forward and scoop it into my hands. It calms down hearing my heartbeat.

"Need to wash you up, little Toma."

"What the fuck, Jennifer?" Carly yells, as does my inner voice. She steps in and slams the lid shut, then presses it around the edges to make sure it's sealed. "You can't be serious."

"You're not my boss," I tell her. While this is true, I have no doubt the higher ups will side with her over me. And not just because my behaviour is unhinged. Unfortunately, Chief Medical Officer Ann is at the door, and she *is* my boss.

Ann puts her hand on my shoulder. "We need to talk, Jen."

It's only then that they notice Toma is alive. Ann withdraws her hand and stares at it. A swathe of blood-coated hair droops to the side revealing its pink eye.

"What . . . ?"

"I found it in the bin," I said.

"Let's go to my office. But wash up first."

In her office, Ann smiles, offers me a seat and some tea. I sit down, and take a sip. I can see the stress in her brow and shoulders.

"What's going on?" she asks me.

"I don't know."

"What is that?" she peers at Toma who stares back at her and makes a sound like someone clearing their throat.

"A . . . new organism?" I offer. And it's true.

"How did you know it was in the bin?"

"Just a hunch."

"Jennifer, you're not really working with me. No-one just digs around in there without reason. I can have you suspended. Could you hand it over? I want to have a look."

I hold Toma tighter—I know I have no reason to be

protective of the thing. But I am. It's unlikely Ann is going to let me take it home with me. But it's equally unlikely that she'll hurt it.

Reluctantly, I let the freshly cleaned Toma down onto the desk. It plods awkwardly around and knocks over a cup of pens. This frightens the poor thing, and it scurries back towards me.

"It doesn't have an anus and its mouth is hardly functional," Ann remarks, pushing it onto its back and placing her finger against its front hole. "It's hard to believe such a thing can survive on its own. Does it have lungs?"

She's right. Toma's structure defies all logic, yet it stands before us anyway.

"What are you going to do with it?" I ask eventually.

"Well, I'd say it's newsworthy. I'll see if we can keep it in the old fish tank, then contact the new stations."

"Should I be there? To make a statement?" I pick up Toma again and pet its hair.

Ann doesn't bother hiding her discomfort seeing the way I treat Toma. "I don't think you need to. Maybe it's better if you take a few days off."

I really won't be able to take it home with me. I leave it on Ann's desk.

⚧

Why did it start in my house? Perhaps it didn't. It makes more sense that this phenomenon is connected to me. Comes from me. Maybe that is why I am so protective over Toma. I get out my old microscope and extract a sliver of my own skin.

The truth is more wonderful than I could have anticipated. The little sliver of my skin under my home microscope shows all the hallmarks of the wall finger; the nucleic processes, growth in what should be dead. It could be that it was transferred to me by whatever was living in the wall, but I believe it's even better than that.

I am the origin. The next stage of human life—no, of all life on earth—begins in me.

Am I worthy of this? It's not like I ever amounted to much. A burnt-out doctor like millions of others. I tried to make my mark in so many ways before. Art house movies, journalism, a brief stint at a prestigious laboratory.

It's not a question of worth, though. Was life worthy of originating in the first place? How could it earn its existence? It's all luck, and it's all inevitable. The guilt drains out of me, replaced with appreciation of my fortune.

A ringing startles me. It's Will. He's been trying to call for ages. Sorry, Will, I've been so caught up. But I answer him now. "Hi, babe."

"Are you okay?" he asks. "I'm on my way back now."

"That's great. Everything is okay. The hand is fine. It's me."

"Pardon? I hope you're not still in the house," he says. I can hear people talking in the background. He's on a train.

"Will, would you still love me if I was the next stage of life on Earth?"

"Babe, what?"

"You heard me. The hand is *me*. My limits have been broken. I'm so excited I don't even know what to feel." I hope he hears my lips curl into a smile. I'm sure he hears the quiver in my voice. "I'm not sure you understand but think about it. I hope you can because not many people loved who I was before even and I'm sure less will now—but I won't hold myself back for anything."

Will breathes. He's still there. My heart is racing, faster than it did even when Carly caught me. "You've always been like that. You'd never let anyone hold you back. Whatever this is, it's not any different. I love you."

"I love you too," I tell him and hang up. I don't have it in me to continue this conversation right now. Besides—there is still a lot to do. I poke the plump clingfilm on my desk. Feeding it sugar water helped it grow but I think it would have grown anyway. Whatever I'm made of now is resilient. I'm sure Toma will be fine.

Cells differentiate by locking down epigenetic modifications. They roll down the Waddington landscape, specialising more and more, going deeper until they can no longer be what they were before. They voluntarily give up their potential for the greater good of the organism. I have done that too. It is why my movies have never seen the light of day, why my research sits unpublished in my computer, why I spend my nights merely recovering from days.

But now my cells have freed themselves. They can be what they want—what I want. Within each of them is limitless potential and I am made of trillions of them. So why should I, a population of infinities, constrain myself?

It's too nice of a day to go to the psychiatrist. The sun is at its peak and a gentle breeze complements its heat. I put on sunscreen although I doubt I need it, then head out the house with a back filled with bloody water bottles. I start in the park, squirting bits of myself into the flower beds, and roots of trees. I dump half the contents of a bottle into the lake. Some people stare—but they have no idea what I'm doing.

Next, I head into town. I squirt bits into the sewers, but I expect I've already gained a hold there. Still, it does no harm.

I reach Natwest, discreetly squirt my liquids onto the carpet. Perhaps not as discreetly as I hoped.

"What are you doing?" a security guard says.

"Nothing, just thinking about switching banks."

"Do you mind explaining what you're doing with that suspicious liquid?" He sounds so polite.

"You wouldn't get it, I'll leave." I don't push my luck. I'm out of there before any more can be said. I go through all the places people need, the vital organs of the city. The grocery stores, pharmacies, the outside of the police department. I'd also go to St. Joans but they clean too frequently and thoroughly. I'd have no chance to grow there. This is enough for now. The sun is setting.

Will gets home and knocks on the door so hard I feel bad for the hinges.

"Are you okay, Jen?" he asks, I hear him drop his bags.

"Just fine," I say from the living room. "Come, my darling. I've had a wonderful day. I am just attending to Smiles right now." I diligently brush the teeth in front of me.

Will freezes when he enters the living room and sees the thing hanging from the ceiling; a terribly long neck, at the end of which is a squashed head. It has no features other than a mouth of ruler-straight, brilliant white, dentist impressing teeth. Unfortunately, teeth are obscured by toothpaste foam and my own hand so Will cannot admire them fully.

"I . . ." Will says. "I'm not sure what's going on." But my boyfriend is curious—that's one of the things I love about him. So, he comes forward and walks around to get the full picture of Smiles.

"It's all me, babe," I tell him. "They're my cells."

This calms him down a bit. He even reaches out to feel Smiles who leans into his touch. I slide my hand over his and give him a kiss. "I've missed you," I tell him.

"I missed you too," he says. "I'm still adjusting."

"That's okay," I tell him.

We go cuddle on the couch.

Toma is on TV. It's doing okay, in the fish tank as expected. It's doubled in size since I saw it yesterday. Ann tells the news reporter how a staff member found it in the biological waste bin. They say they're trying to find out who it came from, but there are no records of recent surgeries. Apparently, there are already requests for samples and to see it in person.

When he's calm enough, Will turns down the TV volume and brings up the main issue: "I'm not sure this is going to last. This is the kind of thing the government will get involved with. What if they take you away and I never see you again?"

"Do you think they could?" I grin and leap to my feet. "All this happened over a few days." I gesture to the house, to the finger in the kitchen, Smiles in who has retreated into its hole, and the clingfilm on the coffee table. "Could they keep up with me, if I kept growing, and spreading?"

"Maybe not," Will says. He takes my hand. "But maybe they can. Humans have driven species to extinction before. Besides, it sounds hard, having to fight everyone all the time."

"I fight everyone all the time anyway," I tell him. "The only difference is that I now have a chance."

"Is that what you want?" he asks, wrapping his arms around me.

"More than anything," I tell him. I look into his eyes. He wipes the sweat from my brow. When did I get so warm?

"Then I'll help you. We can take parts of you far and wide. There's another conference in Japan soon."

"Oh, you're so . . . sweet," I say, the word dragging. My throat tightens. Will holds me upright but ultimately falls back onto the couch, my lips still pressed into his.

My lungs are filled with something.

"I want you to be part of this," I tell him. Except I don't so much as tell him as spew the ichor of my lungs and throat into his mouth.

"It was funny," I tell Will as he gets out of the shower. I stare at the photos he took earlier. Where my tonsils should be—although they were long since removed—are some new dark, throbbing glands. I give Will his phone back.

"Ha ha," he says and pats my head. "Just . . . give me a warning next time, okay?"

As soon as he sits down, I get a call on my phone. It's Ann.

"You're ill," she says. "And you know it."

"What are you talking about?"

"The teacup you drank from was growing something. A little patch of skin where your lips touched it. We had to burn it. We're going to have to quarantine the entire hospital. What even are you?"

"Oh, you're confused," I tell her. "I'm not ill. Something of a miracle has occurred inside me."

"You should come in. I've contacted the health protection team. Either we'll retrieve you at your home, or you can quarantine at St. Joans where the equipment is already available. I know you'll do the right thing."

"No, I just—" I try to say. "Wait, you burnt the tea cup. What about Toma?"

"The thing you found? Someone came and took it away." Before I can say anything Ann hangs up. Moments later, I hear the crunch of car tires on gravel.

The Health Protection Team, accompanied by several police officers, knocks on the door. "Hello?" they ask. "Is anyone in? We're looking for Ms. Jennifer James."

The door is unlocked but the lights are off. Someone figures this out and I hear it creak open from my little hiding place behind the couch in the lounge. The lights turn on in the main hall, then two people (one police, the other I assume HPA), step into the lounge.

"Just leave me alone," I say. "I'm not ill and I haven't done anything."

"Jennifer? It's okay. We're just going to take you to the hospital."

"Like I said, I'm not going. Don't take another step further, or there will be consequences."

The lounge lights flash on. I look up at the ceiling. There's a hole where Smiles came out of—but no Smiles in sight.

"Are you threatening an officer—" the man says. He steps forward. Smiles drops down from its hole, grinning. The man screams and backs away. He immediately calls into his radio. Smiles knows he's a threat. It swings itself back and forward with erratic movements, building momentum, until eventually it slams itself into the officer's face. Both heads cave in—a handful of white teeth scatter. Smiles will recover. It's resilient.

"Thank you," I tell Smiles.

The other person runs out of the room. A few moments later I hear yelling and then the radio on the floor crackles on. "Requesting backup. We don't know what we're dealing with but it just took Charlie down."

I pick up the radio and head out into the garden. Someone spots me and just as soon all three of them are running out but not before the finger (in fact an array of fingers) bursts out the hole and blocks the path. I see something snake its way out of the sink too—I hear it hiss and spit a stream of something. Steam rises from the spots where its projectile landed.

I turn the radio on. "Don't bother me. Seriously, don't."

I gracelessly vault over the garden fence and sprint down the block to where Will is waiting. I know my house can take care of itself now. I only feel bad that we never got to break Toma out.

We're almost at Heathrow when the first bits of news start dripping in. They're being surprisingly forthcoming with info—there are photos of my house, taken from the outside. They catch glimpses of the finger and of Smiles. They know it's related to Toma in the hospital and the weird fleshy growths that appear in the park trees.

The article mentions all the methods they have of eradicating me. Poisons, fire, even radiation.

I laugh. This is how they see me. I'm a flesh monster corrupting the ordinary world. I will never be able to change their mind.

That's why I won't give them the chance to eradicate me. I'll spread further and faster than they can cope with because I will not be held back from being all that I'm capable of. From being the world.

A BRIEF HISTORY OF THE SANTA CARCOSSA ARCHIPELAGO

BITTER KARELLA

IT WASN'T EASY to get the black eggs. Plenty of people were talking about the black eggs, of course, in Discords and chats, and everyone had a friend who knew a guy who knew a guy who could get you the black eggs, but Karen was the first person that Echidna had met who'd actually tried them.

"I eat one every morning," Karen said. "You just mash it into a paste and spread it on toast so that it goes down easier. And everything they say? 100% true. Look!" Karen touched her slender hand to her alabaster throat, downy and smooth, as proof. She laughed a high-pitched tinkling laugh that set Echidna's nerves on edge.

Echidna didn't like Karen. They fucked once, years ago, and Echidna remembered that Karen made awful fake little theatrical gasps the whole time that set Echidna's teeth on edge. That was the last time she'd fucked anyone at all.

Karen opened her refrigerator and pointed. Several evil black spheres sat in the egg rack. Each one shimmered like an oil slick on wet asphalt, a swirling black yolk encased in a clear sac.

"What are these?" asked Echidna.

Karen laughed that fake laugh again. "For beauty, sweetie."

"Yeah, I fucking know. I mean . . . What are these? What lays them?"

Karen smiled and laughed her tinkling laugh yet again as she plucked an egg from the rack. She placed her lips against the wobbling orb and sucked; it instantly popped down her throat. She sputtered and coughed. "I don't know, honey. Some sort of fish."

"Must be a pretty fucking big fish to lay eggs like this."

"Hmm." Karen hummed noncommittally as she closed the fridge door without offering any to Echidna.

"Where do you get them?" asked Echidna.

"I know a guy who knows a guy," said Karen. "And, honey, don't worry. He's very respectful."

The guy that Karen's guy knew worked at the Ranch 99 mall. Specifically, he worked by standing outside a very specific door, right between a Jollibee and a store that sold anime wall scrolls, a door that Echidna has always assumed was a janitor's closet.

Now she got a better look at him on this visit. He was tall and slim and wearing a neatly tailored suit. His head was shaved and she could see the swirly greens and blues of his tattoo sleeves peeking through the cuffs of his shirt as he adjusted his neck tie conspicuously. Was this a mob thing or something? That seemed way too melodramatic for real life. Echidna wandered past him without stopping, turned the corner, did a loop, and nonchalantly wandered back. She was being as inconspicuous as possible, but this time he noticed her.

He crossed his arms. "You want something, pal?"

Echidna bristled. People assumed, from her black nails and her peeling leather jacket and the way she shaved only one side of her head, that she was a badass and that was good because it meant they mostly avoided her. But now this guy was calling her bluff, so she'd have to act the part.

"Karen said you got the black eggs?" Might as well be direct, thought Echidna. She braced herself for whatever response that would elicit. Inside her jacket pocket, her fist clenched around her car keys between her knuckles like the spikes of a mace. She wasn't good at fighting. The last fight she'd been in was when her father busted her nose when she was 14. But she was slippery and if she kept her wits, she knew she could keep ahead of this guy.

"Yeah. Yeah, I thought you might be lookin' fer that." She felt his gaze slide unpleasantly over her thick eyebrows, her square jawline, the scalp visible between the strands of her long scraggly hair. He snorted and opened the door for her. There was a narrow staircase beyond. "Go on in."

She stepped past him, her body tensing as she expected him to lunge out and grab her but he didn't move. He pulled the door closed behind her.

At the top of the stairs, there was a narrow hallway lined with doors, each one labeled in some indecipherable foreign language. At the far end of the hall, a single door stood open. Inside the bare white room, a plump girl with short spiked dark hair sat behind a folding table with a big Styrofoam cooler. There was a faded poster on the wall behind her with palm trees silhouetted against a tropical sunset with the words "Visit Santa Carcossa."

"Hey!" said the plump girl, smiling widely. She stood up and her baby doll T-shirt slid up over her gut, revealing a tender slab of feminine pudge hanging over her belt. She tugged it down again, blushing sweetly. "Gosh, hi! I'm Stephanie! Wow, you're so pretty! Look at you! You must have great genes, Miss . . . ?"

Oh shit, thought Echidna, she's hot. Her eyes strayed to the girl's soft middle. Echidna wasn't expecting this. "Echidna."

"Oh my god, really? I *thought* there was a connection!" The girl clapped her hands in delight. "That's so awesome. I like it. It's beautiful, yet dangerous. It fits you. I saw you and I immediately thought, wow, look at her. So brave! I have so much respect for what you do, just putting yourself out there like that. Just being you! Can I see?"

Echidna was too startled to react when the girl reached across the table and stroked her cheek.

"Wow, so soft! You have *such* a beautiful face," gushed Stephanie. "You could be a model."

Echidna tried hard to ignore the pudge around her middle, which had eased into view again when she raised her hand. Her navel was deep and dark and Echidna could imagine probing it with her tongue. "Um. Thanks. Sorry, Karen said you had . . . ?"

"Oh, a friend of Karen's!" Stephanie laughed, popped the Styrofoam lid off the cooler, and motioned for Echidna to look inside. It contained a dozen eggs bobbing in a pool of melted ice. Echidna thought she saw movement within.

"Don't worry, they're fertilized," said Stephanie. "We wouldn't try to sell you duds."

"What the fuck."

Stephanie smiled and nodded. "Yeah, I know, it's kinda gross. But the results are amazing. Black eggs have been a closely guarded beauty secret among Hollywood elites for decades, so we're really excited to finally make this classic beauty treatment available to the public for the first time."

Echidna nodded. She felt her body sag with a combination of relief and disappointment. Karen made this whole thing sound like it would be a drug deal. But after dealing with that bouncer downstairs, it was kind of a relief to find out she was just gonna get an extremely normal sales pitch, even if this girl was giving her major chaser vibes.

"What lays them?"

Stephanie smiled, linked her arms behind her back and swayed girlishly back and forth. Her full chest swayed. "No one's ever asked that. All our black eggs are humanely harvested."

"Yeah, but what lays them?"

Stephanie blinked as if she'd never considered the question.

Echidna hesitantly plucked one of the black spheres from the tub. It was encased in a clear gelatinous sheath that stuck to her fingers. She looked at Stephanie for guidance.

"I can tell you. Most people don't care, but you . . . you're different. But I can't just tell anyone, you know, we can work something out. I mean, if you're down?"

Karen knows where I am, thought Echidna. If anything happens to me, Karen knows. Not that it would do any good.

"I'm down."

Stephanie squealed and bounced in place. Then her voice got husky, commanding: "Close the door."

This is so stupid, thought Echidna, I'm gonna get myself killed. The room felt way smaller with the door closed. She had to be careful. That bouncer downstairs knew she was up here. He could come busting through the door at any moment. Stephanie might have some way to call him up here. Shit. Was this a set-up?

". . . Not like you, though," continued Stephanie. "I saw you and I thought, oh my god, she is *so* pretty, she must have great genes. I thought to myself, what a beautiful girl. What a great repository of genetic material."

No one had called her a great repository of genetic material before. Echidna rather liked it, but she was still thinking about that bouncer. If he came rushing up, she could get in one good shot, that was all she would need, enough to knock him off kilter and then she could get out.

"Right."

"Not like me. I don't have good genes to pass on."

Stephanie, with her round face, her soft fluffy arms, her wide hips, her chubby belly that slopped over her jeans, her heavy breasts that pressed against the fabric of her shirt with enough insistence that Echidna could discern the outlines of her brassiere; She looked so soft and feminine that Echidna couldn't help but feel a stirring. It had been a while.

"What about your man downstairs?"

"Kenny knows what I like," said Stephanie. "He's not gonna bother us. I used to do this with Madeleine. And Ashley too."

"Uh huh."

"Oh, those are my exes, sorry. They're not around anymore, don't worry about them. They were like you, you know? I just have so much respect."

Echidna wished she would shut up. It was a good thing she was so hot or this would be painful.

Stephanie yanked her shirt over her head and released her bra in one fluid motion; Echidna watched Stephanie's tits swing free and felt her dick stir.

"Oh shit. Fucking hell."

Stephanie approached her and rubbed her chest playfully against Echidna. She ran her finger along Echidna's chin. "Shh. You belong to me now, okay? I'm gonna make you part of me. Do you understand?"

Okay. So she was into kinky roleplay. Maybe this wouldn't be so bad. Echidna had fucked her way out of a few bad situations before. This would be fine. Her breath quickened as Stephanie slid her chubby little hands up under her ratty T-shirt and cupped the nubs of her budding breasts. Stephanie propped herself up on tip toes and brought her mouth close, lips parted. Echidna didn't resist the invitation. It felt so good to come together; It had been so long since she was with anyone, since she had felt the warmth of another body against her skin. Echidna shrugged off her leather jacket and didn't flinch as she heard it hit the floor.

"Every human is an island," whispered Stephanie into Echidna's mouth. "Each of us alone in our own heads."

Echidna didn't care much for philosophy. Her shriveled dick was twitching in her skirt, waking from its long hibernation. Stephanie put her free palm against it, gently cradling the shaft and balls through the vinyl fabric.

"But we don't have to be. When people fuck, it's the one time that we come together, isn't it? Those borders disappear. For most people, at least. But I can make them disappear completely forever. Squat down. You know what to do."

Echidna squatted down until she was level with Stephanie's crotch and pulled apart the fly of her jeans. It parted with a soft grating sound. Echidna tugged at her panties, exposing the chubby girl's bush ensconced in the cozy little crevasse under her belly. Stephanie inhaled deeply, sucking air between her teeth.

"You want to know about where we get the black eggs?"

Echidna mumbled, her breath hot against Stephanie's lips. Why was this girl still talking?

"Do you know about the Santa Carcossa Archipelago? That's okay. I'll tell you. It's a chain of uninhabited islands in the South Pacific. Not much lives in the shallows. Scientists think it's because currents in the South Pacific Gyre block nutrients from reaching the area. By contrast, the depths of the Santa Carcossa Trench have yielded abundant and unique sea life."

How does she keep talking, thought Echidna, but her thoughts were dulling with lust.

"So in 1979, a professor from the University of Hawaii led the last scientific expedition to investigate the Santa Carcossa Trench, just one year before the islands were closed off. Over several months, he made four dives, reaching a combined total of 20,000 feet below sea level in a bathysphere of his own design. Much of the sea life that he observed hasn't been independently verified, making him the only person to ever describe creatures like the Harlot's Progress (*Ogcocephalus meretrix*), the Translucent Ghast (*Lophius exspiravit*), and the Double Decapod (*Macrocheira geminae*). Hmm. Yes. Keep doing that."

Shut up, thought Echidna. She sounded totally different now, all of her girly bubbliness drained away and replaced with a professor's drone. Echidna's tongue slurped deep into her cunt. Stephanie's hands closed tightly on her shoulders. The endless babble should have been a mood killer, but Echidna only felt herself getting hotter and harder. Her dick was raging inside her skirt.

"He also mentioned seeing a thereunto unknown fish drifting through the bathysphere's light beams. A bloated gelatinous orb, floating aimlessly like so many fish down there, a nomad on the current, content in its vegetable bliss, trailing several fan-like paddles that the professor at first assumed to be fins. On later recollection, though, he changed his opinion that they were, in fact, gonads. Hmm. Don't stop. Now, funny thing; certain species of trench fish, in which the males are very tiny and the females are very large, have adopted a peculiar and loathsome mating strategy: The males bite at the female's flanks, locking their teeth in like parasites and hanging there until their flesh fuses, until the female's capillaries reroute themselves to circulate through the bodies of their tiny hitchhikers, until the useless male bodies wither away into nothing and all that's left is a pair of mindless gonads pumping the female with seed and fertilizing her spawn. Technically, I suppose the male is dead, then, since his body dies. But his balls endure, kept boiling and pumping by the flow of his mate's blood."

Echidna moved her face from Stephanie's crotch and pulled her hands away from Stephanie's middle. They peeled away with a sucking sound and Echidna felt a thick gluey sludge sticking to her fingers.

"Oh my god," she breathed. "You're fucking kidding me."

"Hmm, don't stop, Echidna. Please. Keep doing that. Keep doing that and I'll keep talking."

Echidna leaned back in, burying her face between Stephanie's legs again and licking.

"Let me start from the beginning. Yes. Right there. The chain of events that led to this moment began a century ago and across the globe. The first ship to anchor on the islands was the *HMS Valiant*, a British whaling vessel sailing out of Honolulu with a mostly Chinese and Filipino crew, in 1825. Blown off course by an unseasonal typhoon, the ship put to shore on an unknown island; since the ship made landfall on St. Carcossa's Day morn, the captain christened the island with an appropriate name. The captain, Thomas Beckett, kept extensive notes in the ship's log about their visit to the island, an invaluable resource for later researchers. He described the 'ghostly white beaches laced with ribbons of unnatural black sand,' and wrote that the interior was covered in 'unusual vegetation' that was 'uncharacteristic for the region, devoid of wildlife other than some few snails of a tremendous size.' Most importantly, for our purposes, was that the shores were littered with the bodies of 'creatures which we at first thought to be turned inside out by the same gale which forced our landing here, but upon closer examination we found the poor wretches to be in their natural condition.' Oh. Oh. Mmm. That's good.

"Beckett, of course, knew little about the ocean depths or bizarre creatures that populate the deepest of the Pacific trenches. He had no way of knowing that the same typhoon that stranded his ship on the island would have churned the waters so that some of these monsters would rise to the surface. Now you probably know that the creatures of the depths live under tremendous pressure, so much that for many the weight of the water is literally what holds them together—and that the lower pressure of the shallows might cause such creatures to burst apart. What he was seeing, of course, was perfectly natural. But he didn't know that. Oh yes, God. Keep going. Faster.

"Hunger eventually overcame their revulsion, so the crew cooked some of the storm's bounty in a large bonfire on the beach. Beckett reported that the fish had a 'greasy, charred quality to their flesh, strange but not entirely unpleasant.' The ship was quarantined to contain some unknown disease upon return to Hawaii. Beckett does not appear in any further nautical records from the time period, and the HMS Valiant was shortly thereafter decommissioned and sunk at sea."

"You're delicious," slurred Echidna. Her head was swimming and she felt woozy; she was only dimly aware of the details to Stephanie's story. She was ravenous for Stephanie, her whole body was on fire and she was burrowing deeper and deeper into her new lover. She wanted to be inside this beautiful fat body, to be completely subsumed into this flesh.

"I know, I have that effect. Keep going." Stephanie looked down at her, plucking wet strands of Echnida's hair where it plastered against her face. Stephanie's body was soft and fleshy and so much smaller than Echidna. She smelled beautiful. It was affecting her mind, but she was sure that she would still want this even if she was sober. Her body was healthy, it could live for years, decades, but she couldn't stand the thought of that. She wanted it gone, every reminder of it subsumed and swallowed into Stephanie. "Do those fish . . . do they die when their bodies wither? Or are they just . . . inside . . . ?" She didn't care about the answer; she already knew what she wanted.

Stephanie pulled her head close, burying Echidna's face in her stomach. "My flesh will be your universe."

Echidna was still fucking. She should have checked the clock on the wall when they started, just so that she could have some sense of the time passing but, as it was, she had no clue how long this had been going on. Stephanie was asleep now, her breathing deep and steady. She was exhausted after the frenzy of their coupling and eventually she grew bored, stopped talking and dropped into slumber, even as the smell of her in Echidna's nostrils and the maddening softness of her body compelled Echidna to continue. Echidna didn't know how much time had passed. She continued to grind her dick against Stephanie's ass, spilling so much watery jizz down her ass crack that the skin on her cheeks was growing red and chafed. It was almost a relief when Echidna finally rubbed her dick so raw and bloody that it just slopped off. She barely noticed. She kept humping, of course, but all she did was smear blood over Stephanie's ass until her skin started to creep over her thighs and then she couldn't do that either. The blood and jizz and ichor formed a thick butter that held them together, tighter than any lovers had ever come together before.

She licked the lump on Stephanie's left shoulder, the patch of loose red skin that Echidna somehow knew was once Madeleine, and it shivered and tightened in response. Her hand snaked around Stephanie's thighs, fingers lightly brushing over the lump on her hip that Echidna somehow knew used to be Ashley. It was important to remember that they were still here, gone in body but still within her. Echidna moved her hand over her lover, exploring the chub around her middle, the vast expanse of her thighs, the damp dark between her legs. A touch between the thighs roused Stephanie from her sleep, and she breathed softly "There!" She took Echidna's hand in her chubby little fingers and guided her where she needed to go. She was ready again. Echidna knuckled her clit with renewed gusto.

That was the way they went for days: Stephanie would sleep when she tired, wake when she was rested and Echidna would rub and kiss and fondle the whole time, whether she reacted or not. There were moments when the fog lifted, when Echidna might stop for a moment and contemplate her ruined dick or the wet sticky film across her chest and belly that made it harder and harder to keep moving, but then she would inhale and the musky scent of Stephanie would compel her to continue. It was better that way, because in those brief moments of lucidity, when she could see what was happening, what was becoming of her, the panic would set in and she would flail enough that the clear film would tear.

"Shhh," said Stephanie, still lying still on the floor, facing away from her. She must have felt Echidna's heart start to jack hammer. "It's fine. There's nothing to be scared of. My flesh is your universe."

Echidna's voice was squeaky and hoarse; it sounded like a smoker's croak. "I'm scared . . . I'm scared . . ."

"I didn't finish telling you about Santa Carcossa, did I?"

"I'm scared . . ."

"I told you about the *HMS Valiant*, right? Fascinating stuff, isn't it? Don't you just feel that delightful chill running down your spine as you ponder what mysterious disease infected its crew? Of course, your mind goes to those strange fish, doesn't it? The answer is obvious. Luckily, subsequent events may shed some light on the nature of the *HMS Valiant's* fate.

"History intersects again with the islands a little over a full century later during World War II, when they were briefly occupied by the Japanese military to harangue Allied forces stationed at New Guinea and the Solomon Islands. I say *briefly* because the base was abandoned after an outbreak of a mysterious illness, contracted by consuming—you guessed it—Santa Carcossa trench fish. The sickness was characterized by hallucinations, dry mouth, and extreme thirst. In its final stages, a translucent gelatinous film develops around the mouth and eyes, creating a waxy seal, followed by death. Those few who did survive their encounter with the sickness reported long-term after effects like cold sweats, watery discharge, and erectile dysfunction, although it's hard to say anything concrete since the Imperial navy kept a tight lid on the whole situation, and, if the information hasn't yet been lost in the intervening century since the war, no one seems particularly keen to share it. Keep going.

"My grandfather served on Santa Carcossa. I don't

know the details. He didn't talk about the experience much, as was the way of men of his generation, and he spoke even less of it after my mother was born. I was under the impression that it was not a clean birth. Because it turns out that the survivors . . . came home with a new ability. Besides the erectile dysfunction and the watery discharge, I mean. And that new ability's been passed down. Do you understand? You do, don't you? I know what you want."

Echidna was too tired to keep humping. She wanted to continue, her ruined crotch burning yet with unfulfilled desire. She would never stop feeling this way. But it was getting hard to move, her joints were freezing and her skin was crackling. As gooey as the process was, she felt dry, chapped and used up.

Echidna awoke when Stephanie felt a sudden pain in her belly, so intense that Echidna could feel it in her balls, spasming up her spine. She didn't know how long she was asleep. She must have finally dozed off for the first time in days. Stephanie shifted her bulk and propped herself up on her elbows. Echidna's legs and crotch were stuck, but she didn't have the strength to cling on, so her spine arched backwards, her arms flailing, and she expelled a puff of breath through her nostrils. It was all she could do. Her vocal cords were brittle and snapped, her mouth glued shut by ichor. But she didn't need to say anything, Stephanie could feel her pain and fear as a sudden spike of adrenaline blasting through her system.

"Echidna, it's okay," she said, and Echidna felt gentle hands cradling her, pressing her face back into the paste of Stephanie's back until she stuck there. She couldn't see anything—her eyes had milked over and melted and new skin was cobwebbing over her sockets—but she could still hear. Her thoughts were slow and steady, blinking on and off like a buoy on the vast dark night ocean. She heard a drawer opening and the rustle of movement and then Stephanie was winding soft linens around Echidna's frail body, swaddling her little hitchhiker like a baby in a papoose. Echidna was just a dry husk now, her pain transitory and meaningless, but Stephanie didn't want her to suffer in these final moments of separation. Echidna could still sense that, now more than ever, Stephanie's love was pulsing through her just as surely as Stephanie's heart pumped her own blood into Echidna's body through the new veins that connected them as one. She had never been so sure of anything. Stephanie pulled the linens snug and Echidna breathed again, the faintest whisper of a sigh, but Stephanie could hear and understand. Stephanie stood, a little unsteadily after so many days lying prone, and stumbled across the room and opened the door.

They opened another door. There was a toilet inside.

They plopped on the toilet with a groan, leaning forward so that their forehead touched their knees, and shat out a string of black eggs. They filled the bowl, dropping with wet splats into a gelatinous heap. They tore a wad of toilet paper from the roll and mopped the slime from their cunt. Every week, they dropped eggs—fertilized by Madeleine or maybe Ashley or, from here on out, maybe Echidna, there was no way to tell. Each one the promise of a monster yet to be born.

They stood up and there was a sudden crack; the husk dropped from their back, shattering in two as it hit the toilet tank on its descent. They turned to look at it. They remembered when they were young, when the seventeen-year cicadas came and for a week left their molted shells clinging to every tree in the neighborhood. Echidna's spent shell looked like that. She came out of that—no, *they* came out of that. They kicked it out from behind the toilet. They crushed it between their hands and dropped it in the waste paper basket. They tightened the linen; there was still a wound back there, a wet gristly spot where her junk fused with their back, her tubes now under their skin. They could reach back there and juuuust touch it, so that the skin shifted like a sea anemone closing at a predator's touch.

A knock on the door.

"You alright in there? I heard the door."

It was Kenny. He knew better than to disturb them when they were in process.

"Yeah. It's fine."

"You got a new clutch yet? You been up here three days. Your customer's been getting whiney."

"Customer?" They shifted on the toilet seat. "You tell her to go fuck herself. She'll get her eggs when they're ready."

A pause. "Alright then."

They waited as Kenny's foot falls retreated back down the stairs. They thought about fucking Karen and her fucking smug face when she showed off her refrigerator.

They pushed the flusher and grinned as they watched the eggs swirl down the pipe.

SHOW ME

AMANDA M. BLAKE

WHEN HE FIRST made me his, I could do no wrong. He extolled my perfection to beams of morning sun prying through closed blinds, murmured into rumpled, musky sheets and skin, composed music from the tracing of a finger around the crystal edge of glass tumblers and the tightening, darker flesh of areolae.

He placed me on a pedestal carved by his own hands, and when he took me down to show me off, he held me in gentle arms, interlocked our hands, pressed his lips to my cheek, clasped the back of my neck, pressed the toe of his shoe against mine. No one else could touch me.

I was everything he wanted, so I agreed in gold and in the presence of my family and his friends to love, honor, cherish, and obey. That night, the diamond sliced his chest, consummating my contract in blood as well as flesh that he already knew so well, because that was what we both wanted when I was his and he was mine but we were also our own, with no document to sign my name over to his.

He drew me into his home, merged my money into his, and told me I never had to leave, never had to step foot on the other side of the threshold to do more than take care of him, and as long as I did my duty, he would do his. He took me down from the pedestal and placed me in this box, because he had no more use for a vase that couldn't hold flowers.

As his wife, I can't do anything right.

'God, how can you be so stupid? Mother made breakfast, lunch, and dinner for five sons, and we never left the table hungry. I give you the recipe. I give you the ingredients. I give you the time. But you can't even make a single goddamn meal right. If you were a good wife, you would know how to make me a good meal. No, no, don't stir like that. I'll show you how to do it. See, like this.'

With exaggerated motions and a samurai-mask mouth, he stirs the sauce as his mother taught him—the exact angle of his wrist, the direction of the wooden spoon, how to wait for just the right boil, when to take it off the burner, how to pour it over the noodles—which have to be just the right consistency. A second over or under, and the sacred dish of his childhood is ruined.

I have ruined many dishes, offended many gods, picked up many pieces of ceramic from the floor, mopped up gravy and shreds of chicken from the tile, unboxed pristine white plates to replace what he breaks and that leaves tiny ghosts on my hands—many cuts for the one I gave him, for every scar I leave on memories he put on the pedestal to replace me.

'If you were a good wife, you would know how to keep this place clean. I bust my ass, and all I ever asked of you was to take care of our home. It's a thousand-foot apartment. What the fuck do you do all day? Look at the laundry that hasn't been done. Look at the dishes you haven't cleaned. Look at the beer bottles just sitting on the counter.'

He leaves another bottle on the coffee table and gets another. I take the bottle and put it with the rest before rinsing them out and scrubbing at the dishes. I ask him for a working dishwasher.

'We have *a dishwasher. She's called a wife. It doesn't*

take that long, and you have all day. Jesus, look at the state of that. Just give it here. I'll show you how to do it.'

I step back, my head bowed and hands behind my back, as he shows me how to make the white ceramic, clear glass, and stainless steel sparkle. Then he pushes me to my knees with a washcloth and tells me to use my fucking eyes while I clean the line of dirt along the baseboards. It better be pristine in the morning, because I wouldn't want him to show me how it should be. I spend all night with a flashlight and a washcloth, wearing down my knees and using tears to catch the dirt when I ache too much to go to the sink.

While he's at work, I do the laundry, put away the dishes, then vacuum the carpets. I collapse onto the couch and think that I should set an alarm to wake up before he gets home, but I fall asleep too quickly, and I wake to the sound of the door slamming, then the metal clink of a belt buckle as he throws his clothes and white coat in the bathroom, the thump of his shoes as they join the rest of his clothes.

'No wonder this place is a pigsty. My mother scrubbed her fingers to the bone to keep a good house while single-handedly raising her five boys. We don't even have children yet. How can I trust you with my sons if you can't take care of a home with just the two of us? Look at these vacuum lines. They're all over the place. Get your lazy ass up and show me how you vacuum. No wonder your mother couldn't keep a husband.'

I ask him to show me how he wants the vacuum lines to look.

'Like this, you fucking brain cell. Like mowing a lawn—nice, smooth, straight, overlapping lines. If you were a good wife, you'd vacuum this way.'

I ask him to show me again. I want to make sure I know *exactly* how he wants it. He shows me through the living room and the bedroom. Then he carries the vacuum back to the linen closet so it doesn't distort the lines.

'Is that so hard? Now, make my dinner. And if you char the chicken again, so help me . . . '

⚧

While he drinks beer and unwinds from his busy day, I crawl through the apartment and clean the baseboards again. I climb the ladder to dust the top of the kitchen cabinets and refrigerator. I pull myself under the bed to wipe away the dust bunnies. I put his clothes out on the top of the dresser.

'You're folding them wrong.'

I fold again, again, again, until he is satisfied. Then he sits on the edge of the bed, brings me to my knees that haven't seen their normal color in months, and guides me to his cock. I do as I have always done, which was more than enough when I carried my own name. But with his brand upon me, he has higher expectations.

'No, no, no . . . Does it look like I'm enjoying this? How could you possibly get this bad in less than a year? You think that because I spare you hard labor that you don't have to put in the effort on the easy jobs anymore? A good wife knows how to please her husband.'

I lower my head with his hand a fist in my hair. He tries to control how I take him in, but eventually he pushes me back in disgust.

'How did you get to be such a fucking failure?'

I stand, my head still bowed, before sitting next to him and lifting my skirt up my thighs. *'Show me.'*

'I've been trying.'

I take his hand and lead him in front of me, then gently pull him down to his knees. I remove my underwear and thread my fingers through his hair until I can make a fist. Then I guide him between. *'I need you to show me how you want it.'*

'It's not the same for a wife.'

'I just need you to show me how. Show me as though it's the same.'

I hold him how he held me, and he closes his mouth over my clit, drawing it in with luxuriant rhythm and relish, the way he tried to make me do to him.

'Like that.' He starts to climb back to his feet.

'Does a good wife not finish?'

A line of suspicion forms between his eyebrows, but his cheeks and lips are flushed and his eyes darker as he meets my more tentative gaze. He lowers himself back between my thighs to show me what he wants.

He brings me to climax, grunts and groans as I tighten my thighs to the sides of his head and pull at his hair, lifting my hips to urge myself deeper in his mouth. Then I take what he has shown me and prove that I have learned his lesson.

But although I am an apt student in the moment, I am the failure that he says I am and must be shown again, and again, and again.

'You look like old carpet. I have the opportunity to fuck so many beautiful women who would kill to be in your shoes. They try to make themselves beautiful, or wish to God they could be. Your clothes are wrinkled, your tits are starting to sag, your skin is so lifeless, and you're getting fat. Is it too much to ask that you take a little pride in yourself and show some appreciation for what I do for you? A good wife would keep herself attractive for her husband.'

He buys me a treadmill and tells me to use it when I'm done in the kitchen in the evenings. I do the exercises he instructs me to while he slouches on the couch, drinks his beer, rests his arm on his soft belly, and watches to make sure my form is correct.

'You call that a push-up? Do I have to do everything for you?'

He shows me how to do a push-up every time I do it wrong. He lays with me on the ground with his feet under the couch as he shows me how to do sit-ups. For every ten minutes I fail on the treadmill, he spends ten minutes showing me how I should run.

But although he shows me with his body how mine should tone, and although there is now less love for him to pinch at my waist, he still slaps the weight of my tits and ass, the pouch of my belly, the cellulite of my thighs, the things that were already mine before I was ever his.

He forces a mirror in my face as I'm preparing to join him for Sunday morning church. *'You don't even bother putting on mascara anymore, do you? Mother always wore a dress for my father, always made sure that when he came home or when she went out, she looked her best, because she represented him. She didn't want to disappoint or let him down. You disappoint me.'*

'What do you want me to do?'

He pulls out the cocktail dress I wore for him at the rehearsal dinner. He finds the makeup I once used all the time, the kind that he said made me look natural instead of like a whore or a corpse. When I sponged on too much foundation, he snatched it from my hand. *'No. Not like that.'*

He practices on his own face until he makes himself look more natural than nature, until his eyes pop and his skin is clear as matte porcelain, until I kiss him and smear his gloss on my lips. He reaches for the makeup remover, but I rest my hand over his.

'If it's natural, no one ever knows.'

I repeat what he showed me. He zips me into the dress that he chose. Pinches the folds that form when I bend over to put on my shoes.

'A good wife wouldn't let herself be seen like this. Don't you have something to tuck this in? It's not that fucking hard.'

I open the drawer that holds my underwear and shapewear and pull out two of the whale-bone corsets he bought for his pleasure. *'Show me.'*

He laces me in, then I practice on him. Because we're running late for the last service, we leave together, the silhouette of the corset he wears hidden under the jacket.

After the wedding, I never visit him at work, and he never invites me to have lunch with him, lest his colleagues realize what his wife has become since they saw me in white.

But then he brings his work home.

He clears off the coffee table himself, which is enough to make me pause while cooking dinner.

He sets a black physician's bag in the center of the glass top, then sheds his clothes as he heads toward the shower. I have dinner ready for him when he comes out. Although he curls his lip at the roasted salmon, he doesn't deride it for being overcooked or raw like he usually does.

Wariness and relief war in the clenched fists of my chest. When my daily insufficiencies warrant no mention, it means he seeks to right a grander insufficiency. I can barely swallow as I catalogue all the things I've done wrong.

He ruminates in sweatpants and no shirt, staring at me without seeing. I wear my dress and my smile for him, but my cheeks hurt and my lips threaten to tremble.

When he's through, he pushes his plate away and stands. I clear the table without finishing my meal, which I store in the fridge, because he would scold me for scraping it into the bin, throwing his money away. However, I suspect I will be no more inclined to eat it tomorrow, depending on the state he leaves me in tonight.

He opens a soda instead of a beer. My hands tremble, knocking the ceramic harder against the sides of the sink. My gaze remains downcast, but I feel the accusation he keeps to himself.

'Come here.'

I dry my hands and obey, fingers curling inward, tendons like rubber bands stretching taut.

'Take off that stained dress. Take off all your clothes.'

I render myself vulnerable under the unkind canned lighting. He has bedded me before outside of the bedroom, but this doesn't *feel* like the bedroom, where he kneels before me to show how I must please him or where I demonstrate my retention of the lesson.

He opens his physician's bag. Although he is half naked himself, he regards me as though he never left his office.

'All that a husband ever asks from his wife is that she tends the home and gives him something worth coming home to. We've gained some ground on tending the home, but I think we need to take more drastic measures on this ugliness you cling to so stubbornly.'

He pulls out a black pen, with a scent that stings my nose when he uncaps it.

'Here. This needs to be trimmed and tucked. Here. This needs to be smoothed. Here. This needs to be smaller. I have tried to be patient. I have tried to be kind. But no matter how much I show you, you're just too dull and lazy to understand how far a good wife should go.'

He traces my sections like slabs of butcher meat, marks where he will diminish me further. Then he lifts my breasts with the tips of his fingers, sneers at the shadows that form underneath them when he lets them fall again.

'We'll lift you here, of course, but I think you can give me more.'

He pulls out bags of silicone gel in varying sizes and holds them up to my chest, small to large. He chooses a midsize and sets them aside.

'A good wife will do anything *to look good for her husband. You want to be a good wife, don't you? You promised you would. You swore to me.'* He caresses my face with blunt nails, then clicks his tongue as he strokes under my chin and closes his hand softly around my neck. He retrieves his pen to make a few more marks.

The leather bag creaks as he reaches in. He pulls out a scalpel and brings it to my cheek. *'Tomorrow, I'll have you under my knife, but tonight, I'll have you under me. Let's see what you've learned.'*

He wakes when I switch on the lights—not just the overhead lights on the bedroom fan but the lamps as well, including one I brought in from his desk in the living room corner, the halogen light that hurts to look at directly but that beams clarity onto his body stretched out before me.

Over my nakedness, I wear my apron. I give him nothing to cover his. He splays on our bed like a frog in a dissection pan, his ankles and wrists tied to the bedposts with his silk ties—sturdy stripes and patterns overlap to bind him. No matter how he strains, neither metal nor wood groans to hold him.

He bellows, but the gag balled in his mouth stifles his fury, as the neckties still his struggles.

'You said you wanted to help me be a good wife, because I promised that to you. But you know how bad I am at this. You know I need you to show me many times how you want it done.' I lift the physician's bag onto the bed and open it. *'I won't be able to do it until you show me. So, walk me through what you want to do to me. I hope I'll be able to understand, that I'll be able to get it right for you. Show me what a good wife does, how a good wife looks. Would she have this pouch of fat here in the abdomen?'*

He stares up at me. Color rides high on his cheekbones, in his lips, in the whites of his wide, darkened eyes.

'If you show me how to do this right, then I can do it for you, too. I want *to be a good wife. I want to be the* perfect *wife. That's all I've ever wanted. Now, this part of my belly was marked for removal. Am I to understand that this is not attractive?'*

Slowly, he nods. Because what else can he do, if he's to have what he wants?

Just as the gag blocked his bellows, it forces him to swallow his screams when the scalpel slices through.

Blood drips down his sides, but tears drip down his temples. He is stunned by how devoted I am.

Before he unenrolled me from university to be his wife, I took some of the same classes as him, and when I had nothing but time in a thousand-square-foot apartment, I studied the books in his office; the terminology, the theory, the diagrams. My cuts are clean and precise from every bird I have carved as he has taught me. I let little blood soak through the mattress by using clotting gauze, and I sew a perfect stitch from all the clothes he has taught me how to mend.

I have worked *so* hard to comprehend what he wants from me, and he helps me understand what is necessary, what I must do, everywhere on his body that I can reach. Then I bring out the sizes of silicone gel and hold them to his chest.

'The midsize will be mine, but if I were like you, these larger ones would make me just perfect. Do you agree?'

In the wake of my devotion, he nods again. He shows me what a good wife would do.

I can tell, as I finish the work he has planned for me, that I instill some pride within him at last. I am nearly finished. He is nearly finished.

I tend to him as he recovers, as is my duty. In the end, there's barely any scarring. When he regains his mobility without too much pain, he shows me how I must maintain myself, and I understand so much better now. I close my eyes in his operating theater, inhale the anesthesia through the mask, and trust his knife, as he trusted mine.

Other than the surgeries I required, for which he only

waited for a steady hand, it takes longer than physical rehab for him to truly recover so that he can resume his practice. I must step outside my Bermuda Triangle of the apartment, grocery store, and coffee shop to support us. It isn't anything like what he brought in, but it's something, and I've started taking evening classes at the local college to continue what I began before accepting the golden shackle on my finger. I have more time for that now, because he knows best how one must tend the home while the other acquires income, and I trust his judgment. I trust him. I finally understand.

Because now he has the perfect wife. And so do I.

MAN OF THE HOUSE

LILLIAN BOYD

FIRST AND FOREMOST, Mr. Ronald Ray Humboldt Jr. will be goddamned if he'll be driven out of his home by some fruity fucking ghost.

Second of all, he ain't likely to find a sweeter deal on a two-story in the Charlotte metropolitan area since the news came out about that little twelve-year-old boy in the dress who ate a gun down in the basement last year.

Third, the singing coming from the basement is starting to work his nerves. A little.

It swirls up through the floorboards of the old blue house in the wee hours while Ronnie Ray is trying to sleep and it nestles like mold underneath the static of phone calls to his fucking wife and it hums in harmony with the wheezy, ancient dishwasher. That same spidersilk contralto every time. Always that same Aerosmith song, the one about fucking a dude who looks like a lady. Or a lady who's really a dude. He can never keep it straight.

Ronnie Ray never liked Aerosmith—that lead singer's wet, pillowy lips always made his gut squirm—and he hated that song way before some little dead boy decided to make it a fucking karaoke classic.

It was all over the news when it happened here a year ago at 221 Whispering Trails Drive, the whole mess leading up to it: The kid's daddy found out he was some kinda queer—one of the transgendereds, maybe, or maybe even the regular kind that just wanted to suck your dick in the men's room—and blew his brains out all over the basement with a little nine-millimeter Glock, then turned himself in, grinning sheepishly about it to the cops who tucked him into the back of a patrol car.

Alex Dearborn, the kid's name was.

The kid's mama moved away after that, to Savannah or Athens or somesuch, and the same hour the cops cleared away all that yellow tape, the house went up on the market for a song. There weren't too many bites, but the ones that did come and check it out didn't stick around long. Ronnie Ray asked some of them what it was that had put them off, and they all did the same song and dance about the Vibes and Energy of the big blue house, all that New Age dogshit. But Ronnie didn't care about any of it—not after everything went to hell with his wife Rhonda. Just because he got a little loaded and did some stuff and she called the cops on him and he got out of the tank to find the locks changed and a big fat restraining order jammed in his face, he needed a place to sleep and he needed it pronto.

And renting wouldn't cut it, either. Ronnie needed to make sure nobody could ever overreact and kick him out of his own place again. After living out of a Red Roof Inn for a couple of weeks and working his magic on those real estate agents with the money he'd managed to sock away before Rhonda went and locked the joint savings account, the place was his.

He hadn't even seen the house before he bought it. Didn't need to.

It was his.

Looking back now, the first night he spent here was when it started going bad.

He had his easy chair, he had a little flatscreen TV he'd

picked up at a yard sale, he ate some Dinty Moore beef stew in a living room lit blue by a news special about the bathrooms at the local mall and the transgendereds wanting to use them. He snorted into the watery gravy when the newsman said some freak got put in the hospital after getting dragged out of a stall in the women's room and catching a whooping from mall security. "That's what you get," he mumbled, and cracked another Keystone Light.

When he stumbled to the first-floor bathroom on his way to bed, bladder aching and beer-heavy, he couldn't get the door open. He rattled the doorknob and banged his shoulder into it, but no joy—every time he made progress shoving it open, some deep-down gust from within pulled it shut, smacking it against his clammy forehead.

Fuck it, he thought, *whatever*, and he went to try the upstairs bathroom. The door opened smooth as butter, but when Ronnie Ray tried to open the toilet, it held fast like concrete had been poured between lid and seat. He strained to lift it in a race against his bladder. He fumbled to drop his zipper and piss absolutely fucking anywhere, but he missed the deadline, drenching himself by the time he got his pants down.

As he shuffled past the mirror on his way out of the bathroom, a cursory glance at his hangdog reflection gave him a start—for a moment, just a moment, he had deep-red lips and thick lashes and a face shaped like a heart. He blinked and leaned in and looked closer, and when he wiped the glass with the flat of his hand, it was just Ronnie's face, the same as it always was. Piss cooled on the backs of his thighs.

That's what you get, the bathroom whispered.

He peeled off his pants and crawled into bed, stinking and sticky, and when his eyes closed, he heard the singing, giggly and faint as a far-off train's whistle.

That fucking song.

"I ain't afraid of you, Alex Dearborn," Mr. Ronald Ray Humboldt Jr. says in the stale cold of the basement the next morning, not sure where to look and landing on the bare bulb hanging from the ceiling. He says it big and sharp like his daddy used to when his mama would talk back and he had to set her straight, sticking his chest out and curling his lip.

"All those other pussies that came here, maybe this ghost shit was enough to scare them off. I ain't them. You hear me? You better get used to me, 'cause I'm staying here as long as I want. I bought this house fair and square. My own money," he barks, his voice rising a half-step.

No answer. The air conditioning rattles and moans through the grates.

"I'm gonna stand my ground. You know what that means, Alex? It means I can do whatever I want in my own home and there ain't no fucking queer," he spits, "who gets to tell me I can't. You died and I didn't. This ain't your house now."

The light bulb twitches at the end of its wire like the protests of a dying spider, then twitches again. Ronnie steps back without thinking about it, swallows hard.

"So quit messing me around. With the doors and the weird mirror shit and that stupid song. You hear? I hate that song."

Slowly, the naked swinging bulb fills with dark, thick red like a bedbug engorging with its stolen dinner. The glass pushes and strains until it bursts and spacks the walls and floor and Ronnie Ray's slack jaw with its ichor. It tastes like cherry soda syrup.

He yelps and hunches and spits it out, wiping his face with his sweaty palms.

That skinny little voice sweeps through the room, tickling the dust and mildew.

I thought you'd like that song. My daddy did.

"We don't do exorcisms here. Sorry," says Pastor Rick of First Baptist Church in Gastonia, in a tone of voice like he's telling a kid who's old enough to know better that the Easter Bunny isn't real and isn't bringing him any jellybeans.

"No, no, come on," says Pastor Johnny of the Church of The Pentecost in Concord, patting Ronnie on the back and nodding to a burly usher to let him know this gentleman might need some help leaving, "you're better off trying the Sacred Heart Church. Down the street. You have a nice day, now."

"Hell yeah, brother, let's send this ghost's little homo ass screaming back to hell," says Assistant Manager Darryl of the Kwik-Go Gas Station & Convenience Store in Fort Hill, formerly Pastor Darryl of St. Peter's Baptist Church in Charlotte for fifteen years until the other church elders made him step down on account of those things he did at that motel over in Boone.

Ronnie Ray found him on an online forum devoted to globalist plots, hidden Satanic influencers, and gender terrorists called Babylon Bound. In the subforum Spiritual Warfare, a post by user RighteousMan14 titled "Drive out the devil's gay demons with the power of Christ . . . . . ." caught his attention, and it promised the goods—ancient texts dating back to the annihilation of Sodom and Gomorrah that boasted the ability to identify, expose, and cast out any unclean spirits of sexual perversion with the bad luck to run across a true-blue badass of God. But the text was written in Sumerian, the post said, and the only person with the biblical learning to know what to do with it was the poster himself.

And damned if RighteousMan14 wasn't a stone's throw from Ronnie over in Fort Hill. All they had to do was meet up at a bar halfway between their houses to discuss the particulars.

"I kinda been waiting for somebody to call me about this, you know?" Darryl says, not looking at the bartender who hands across his opened bottle of beer. "There's all kinds of demonic shit going on now. Ever since the election a couple years ago."

"Is that right?" Ronnie says, hating the way his legs dangle off the barstool without being able to touch the floor.

"Little peckerwoods feel brave now. Like they can just go anywhere, move into people's backyards and stay there. We're a fallen nation," he says, wiping his lips on the shoulder of his button-down and setting his beer down harder than he needs to on the lacquered counter of the bar. "A fallen nation."

"I hear that," Ronnie says.

"And when I heard about it, what happened after that man finally had enough of that shit being in his house, I just knew, boy. Chickens coming home to roost."

"So how's this gonna work?"

"O ye of little faith," Darryl says, smiling slowly, "you just leave that to me."

"I know you by your true name, unclean spirit," Darryl tries booming in the basement, his face lit only by a little camping lantern he holds out in front of his face like a torch in the badlands. Ronnie Ray stands a couple of feet behind him, looking around at the shadows shuddering across the concrete walls for any sign that his tormentor is with them in the buzzy dark. "I name thee Belial, I name thee Adversary, I name thee Unwanted."

The ghost's name is Alex, Ronnie thinks, but doesn't say anything.

"In the name of Christ Jesus, the Prince of Peace, I rebuke thee," Darryl says, reading from a laminated page in a big white binder with a long bullet-pointed list of exhortations in Papyrus font.

"I bind you and cast you out, O Fallen One, O Boy-Whore of Babylon," Darryl continues, doing a little half-wave with the binder, raising his voice some.

"So, uh," Ronnie Ray says, "does it look like it's working, or is—"

"Spirit," Darryl says, sweat glossing his upper lip, "leave this precious man of God in peace and trouble him no more."

Ronnie's flattered by 'precious,' but if he's being honest, Pastor Darryl's losing him. Ronnie'd been expecting some more heavy-duty fireworks than this. Hell, he could read this shit off a page if he wanted to. The words look easy enough. He doesn't know what Sumerian sounds like, but it ain't this. He wonders if he should ask for some kinda discount if that little ghost doesn't show.

"Foul," Darryl says, face purpling, "foul queer, be not here."

The shadows hold impossibly still, like the moment following a surprise marriage proposal. The hum of the air conditioning swallows a lump in its throat and vanishes.

"Foul queer, be not here," he repeats, picking up steam, eyes shining wide and gratified in the light of the camping lantern as the shadows gather from every corner of the basement to settle in a puddle of void straight across from Pastor Darryl.

"Foul queer, be not here," Darryl says, looking over and twitching a come-on gesture at Ronnie with open palms.

Ronnie obliges, his adrenaline shot to the sky as the camping lantern brightens and brightens, illuminating—is that a face, staring from the dark?

Is that a fucking smile?

"Foul queer, be not here!" they yell in messy unison, and again, and again, trying to time it right so that they hit one unified voice together. It feels good to Ronnie, trying to match the cadence of his voice with another man's, making something big and strong together, changing things back to how they're supposed to be.

"Foul," Pastor Darryl begins, chest swelling with the holy cleansing fire of Jesus, when a thousand thick fingers of shadow grip his face and lift him up off the floor.

The lantern tumbles to the concrete with a jumpy clatter.

He howls and thrashes, clutching at the air and kicking at nothing as he rises and rises. The binder full of prayers hangs in the air next to him, rotating in lazy loops. Darryl's mouth hangs open, his tongue lolling big and flat over his chin.

"Shit. Shit," Ronnie says, rushing forward to grab the lantern. He drops it with a cry as it burns his hands, motor-hot.

"Help me. Jesus, please, help me." Darryl dangles like laundry, every muscle in his neck screaming as he scrabbles to pull himself up.

The white binder tumbles open in midair and the pages—hundreds of them, half of them blank—fly up in an arc like a cardsharp's party trick and hover in the air above Pastor Darryl's gaping mouth.

Ronnie cries out as the pages drive themselves in, a stream shooting into Darryl's mouth and down his gullet, crumpling fast and wet as they work their way down him, through him, one after the other. Hot blood bubbles from his mouth before being shoved back in, spitting up out of his nose and running down his cheeks. The thundering ripple of paper downs the last sound he ever makes. Whatever he wanted to say is between him and God.

His belly expands in a sick balloon as it fills, his arms and legs dropping limply as the last page finds its way home, the shadows cradling his body up in the air. Finally, with a sound like a phonebook torn in two by a strongman, Pastor Darryl's gut opens.

He spills his payload of intestines and blood and shit and paper, so much paper, down onto the concrete with a fluttering plop. The rest of his body follows suit a few moments later.

Ronnie, dumbstruck and fixed hard in place, thinks he probably should've run when he had the chance.

The shadows slide down into the floor and up the walls, the white-hot lantern illuminating a pretty, cherry-lipped face as it melts back into the cinderblocks.

Did you like that? the voice hums, soft and sweet.

"I, uh."

Ronnie Ray figures Pastor Darryl must not have known what he was doing, reading out those prayers like that, or else Jesus would've kept him safe, right? He must have done it wrong. Jesus isn't gonna help his ass now. Not after what Ronnie just saw. But he ain't about to make the same mistake—he's a slick sonofabitch who can charm the panties off a nun, and he knows that sometimes, you gotta tell people the sappy shit they wanna hear to get what you want.

And this is his house.

"Listen, I think you and me got off on the wrong foot. When I called you all that stuff before, I was just, you know, I was out of line. Wasn't no call for it. I know that now."

Cool relief washes across him. All he's gotta do is keep talking. He can save this.

In the hot glow of the camping lantern, he can see the shadows on the wall holding their breath, moving at a lazy boil.

"Y'all are born like that, right? You can't help it. You're just born like that."

The ghost must be thinking it over, and Ronnie lets out a breath. Whether or not he can get this fucker taken care of for good with a real bigshot exorcist, this'll at least buy him enough time to get up the stairs and out of the house. He'll lick his wounds at the Red Roof Inn and figure out what to do next. All he has to do is make it out.

"And hell, I may not like that one song, but you sing pretty good."

The bubbling shadows go very still.

"I could get used to it. You got a real pretty voice for a boy," he says, hoping he hasn't overworked it.

Ronnie opens his mouth in what he hopes is a conspiratorial grin—but as his top lip stretches, the shadows shoot between his teeth and enter him in a frozen rush.

The ghost fills him up like a lungful of lake water that just keeps going down. Ronnie Ray staggers, trying to maintain his equilibrium, but he doesn't have to—his legs stay solid as Alex fills them and freezes them into the concrete. He can't move an inch.

Don't hurt me, Ronnie thinks, hoping the ghost can hear from inside him. *Don't hurt me. I'll leave. I swear I'll leave.*

His stomach expands, swollen with ice. He gasps in pain as hands and feet mash against his belly from the inside, puckering his navel like an innertube's valve.

Ronnie's brain spins as he scrabbles to figure out his next move—Cajole? Threaten? Try a few of the prayers Darryl didn't?

But he stops thinking as Alex moves in a cold flash down his body.

No no no God no, he thinks as his dick fills up with ice.

The slit on the end of his pecker winks open gently. With a slow tear, it opens bigger and bigger, peeling apart like string cheese.

Mr. Ronald Ray Humboldt Jr. wants so badly to scream from the pain. He can only manage a small squirm as every nerve ending and blood vessel comes unknit.

The crack in his dick parts him down the middle. The two strips of skin yawn wide as blood soaks the back of his slacks, stretching to wrap around his hips like a belt. With a hard twist, the two flaps whip back to center, weaving themselves into two gushing parentheses where the base of his dick used to be.

It's like you said, Alex says inside Ronnie Ray. *I was born this way.*

Ronnie's head falls down onto his back, his legs kicking the lantern as his legs splay in a wide-open V.

The ghost works through the hole framed by the makeshift lips, widening Ronnie like a tire jack. His hip bones crumple, pulverized. He can feel every rib cracking, sucking in, his spine crumbling as it merges with the slick meat of his organs. Thick ropes of gore squeeze tight through the hole between Ronnie Ray's legs along with whatever's coming out of him.

The last thing he can see emerging from the ruin of his body before the shadows take him is a gorgeous, glowing face.

It's not the face of a boy who's pretty enough to look like a girl through some trick of the shadows.

It's a girl.

Alex Dearborn works her way out of the husk of Ronnie Ray as all that blood sluices off her, cold and new and clean.

In the basement of her house, she sweeps the two men's bodies into a neat jumble of parts in the corner, glides over to the cracked camping lantern, and snuffs out the light.

LOOKING FOR THE BIG DEATH

TALIESIN NEITH

I USED TO spend a lot of time wondering what it would take to get someone to kill me.

This was a funny by-product of numerous mental health issues that I was too stubborn to get treatment for. I was too forgetful to take meds consistently. I didn't like talking about my feelings, so therapy—in person, online, self-help books, journaling—was a non-starter.

The one thing I didn't actually try was killing myself. I didn't want to be alive, but suicide seemed a lot of effort. Too much risk trying to get the reward. If you fuck it up and don't die, you either maim yourself *or* you end up in hospital until you're determined not to be a suicide risk anymore and that fucks up the rest of your life. They don't offer lobotomies anymore, much to my disappointment.

I was a mess of my own making. Big fucking deal. Drank too much, too many drugs, excess apathy. I wouldn't change because that required buying in, and wanting to live.

So instead of treatment, I had intrusive fantasies. I would get the result I want, and it would take all the blame and strain out of it. It's not my fault I got dead, it's their fault. I'm a tragedy, not a basket case or a footnote.

I'd be standing in the kitchen at my mum's whilst she was cooking and wonder what I could say to make her stab me sixteen times. My boss would be walking across the car park at the same time as me, and I'd think: *What if he ran me over?* The stranger on the train platform who stood too close to me could shove me onto the tracks right before my commute.

Turns out, it takes less than you'd think.

My boyfriend and I put up with each other. We had been the only gay kids in our school—I started out his girlfriend, turned into his boyfriend after two years. The two of us stuck together like wolves without a pack, runty bastards who would die in the winter without each other.

We were together for ten years. From secondary school to the moment that he killed me.

He was picking me up late from my favourite pub, and he was fuming. I was sloppily drunk and trying to get a hand down the back of his pants. He bundled me into the passenger side of the car and stormed around to his side. He didn't check that I'd done up my seatbelt before we drove away. It was not the first time he'd been called to pick me up that month.

Here is what they don't tell you about dying: you know it's happening. You might not want to die, you might be praying or wishing not to. You might be thinking about the miracle cure that could save you, or the firefighters with the jaws of life that might free you. You may have blinded yourself so thoroughly to the facts that you don't even realise you're dying. But your body knows. Your body screams it at you.

Mine sang it to me like a pre-funeral dirge as I was jammed through the front window of my boyfriend's car. I could barely feel my legs, still inside, draped haphazardly over the dashboard. My arms were stuck out, reaching over the bonnet, my body suspended strangely by the glass around my middle. My left wrist had snapped dirty, trailing at a strange angle, blood dribbling down the car and bone protruding from torn flesh.

I knew this was it. I felt for so long that death was a

lover I hadn't met yet. Some passersby had pulled over at the accident to gawk. One woman walked around the car to take my intact hand in hers. She told me I was going to be okay.

I was drooling blood at this point, a foamy pink mix with saliva. Blood was in my eyes, dribbling down from my caved-in scalp that glittered with glass in the street lamps. I wasn't in a talkative mood. I think you need a complete frontal lobe for that, and mine was bowing under pressure.

Instead, I breathed at her, a rattling, choking noise, inhaling saliva and retching it back out. My lungs were compressed, one collapsing. A broken rib had slid cleanly into their meat. I had wanted to say *fuck you* to her. I didn't look like someone who was going to be okay. I looked like a cow gone to slaughter.

I saw a video where they're put on a conveyor belt, squeezed down a narrow channel so they can position the cow for someone above to fire a bolt into their head. When the bolt is fired, blood starts trickling out of the puncture wound, but the damn thing isn't beef yet. It's still awake. Still sentient.

Nobody tells the cow that it's going to be okay. It's the slaughterhouse. They hope that the bolt has damaged the brain enough to stop it trying to escape. There are more cows to kill, after all.

I don't know where my boyfriend fit into this crappy metaphor. He was controlling the bolt or the conveyor belt or both. He was not a good boyfriend when I died. He was a useless sobbing lump on the ground, metres away. He could've been another dead cow except he was completely unhurt. That was the magic of seatbelts. Maybe whiplash accounted for how useless he was, but he wasn't the one dying.

There's a point where you stop feeling pain as pain. Dying was the first time I understood the appeal of masochism. Fear and pain and every neuron firing in the throes of impending death transformed into something bright, hot, nearly pleasurable. The slew of new sensations alone was intoxicating. I had never heard anyone scream my name with guilt, with love, with sorrow. Nobody had ever looked at me with such remote sadness as the woman holding my hand, tinged with repulsion for my mangled body.

I had never been still on a motorway at night. It looked so completely endless.

I'm still put out that my boyfriend managed to kill me entirely by accident, instead of something more interesting, like outright homicide or at least killing himself, too. Ironically, it is fucking pedestrian to die in a car crash. He didn't even yank the wheel on purpose—a fucking muntjac deer leaped out in front of his car, and instead of sacrificing it to the bonnet, he panicked. It's tragic, but it's insipid.

At least the lights were brighter. Everything felt like it was building not to something, but to nothing. Dying was being on the cusp of nothing, and when I fell over that edge, all those lights seemed to shatter. I flew in every direction at once. I was gone.

I woke up some hours later in a mortuary cabinet, freezing my bits off, a toe tag pinching at my circulation. I gasped and wheezed and bolted upright, promptly smacking my head off the metal ceiling. It took less than a minute for me to start screaming and thumping my fists, and a very distressed apprentice who had arrived early for work ended up letting me out maybe forty-five minutes after that.

I was scrambling the second the body tray was sliding, until I hit the floor and started shivering. The apprentice was staring at me. All I could think to say was, "mate, I'm fucking naked, don't stare!" and that panicked him enough to send him running from the room. He returned minutes later with clothes in his arms that he threw at me like my pussy was radioactive. In his defence, nobody's ever brought along a dosimeter to check.

The clothes were all a few sizes too big. I held out a t-shirt in front of my body and said, "These aren't mine."

"We had to cut you out of yours," he said, dazed in a way that made him sound half-asleep. "You were practically bisected by the car. You had head trauma, a broken leg, broken wrist. You weren't using your clothes anymore." He took a big gulping terrified inhale. "You were definitely dead. You were so fucked up, oh my god. You don't even look hurt now. Is this your wallet?"

It *was* my wallet, so I took it. I looked at myself carefully as I got dressed. He was right. There was not a scratch on me, not so much as a bruise, but I could remember the strange salty taste of the bloody froth in my mouth, the full body ache, and the moment where all the lights went out.

"Pretty weird, huh," I said, and then I booked it.

The little fucker was clearly too confused and scared to make a grab for me, so I was able to tear out of the mortuary, bursting into the body of the hospital. I stopped to get my bearings and remembered that I'd spent two days bedded in here when my top surgery incisions got infected and I had to be brought in by ambulance. I took a left out of the building, into the car park, past a closed mammogram van, and fled into the woods that surrounded the hospital.

There was no plan. I was making sure I wasn't being followed, running for my new-found life in shoes that belonged to someone who had definitely stayed dead. And what a fan-fucking-tastic second chance I was being given. A second chance at life. Either I was insane, this was all one really shitty prank, or God or Lucifer or what-have-you had seen fit to return me. Me, of all people!

This ultra-positive second chance feeling lasted about two hours until I was in a Gregg's thinking I should at least *try* to eat something. I discovered that I had no appetite at all. Every mouthful felt like forcing something I shouldn't, like I was so full I could never eat again. I wasn't thirsty, either—my mouth didn't run dry, my throat didn't parch. I just . . . was. I existed.

I didn't have so much as a twinge of dysphoric thought. I wasn't worried that my thighs were too big, or my hips too broad.

It was worse than when I'd been alive the first time. I didn't need the apathy of my mind to join my body, but round two decided to make them match perfectly. Perhaps it was a natural path, the single possible conclusion that all of me could lead to. Perhaps when I had been undone, I had been put back together so that all of my pieces fit.

Fuck, it was so boring. I missed dying. I missed how loud it was. When you broke it down it was all noise and sensation, hyperawareness coming from every part of the body straining through its final moments. Not seeing your life flashing before your eyes, but the end of your life slowing down. Gorgeous, sensual detail, every nerve that can spark up doing just that.

I thought I should do it again. Not simply die: be killed. On purpose.

Maybe it would stick this time. Let me into the void that came after and not bring me back. I wondered how it would feel if someone killed me fast, or really slow. I stood a better chance of the former than the latter. I didn't know how to *get* someone to do it, though. How do you start soliciting your own murder?

I turned to message boards. There's some real filth there. I think that's how the gay cannibals from Germany got in touch. That story had always fascinated me and I felt like now I was understanding why. For a while, things were promising, but after a few dozen messages back and forth I realised these were just people hot on the fantasy of murder. None of them had the balls to go through with it. They wanted erotic role play: *baby, tell me how it feels when you die.*

I could have told them, but I wasn't interested in anyone's gratification but my own. Besides, I had limited experience. What if dying from strangulation felt differently to a car crash? What if being shot in the throat hurts in a different way? No one wants an orgasm based on misconceptions.

I spent two months of my non-life coasting with no stability except my phone. I didn't need to sleep anymore. I felt the cold but wasn't bothered by it. I showered sometimes, but it was more out of a sense of obligation. I didn't seem to work right anymore. I thought seriously for the first time about killing myself, but now I wanted audience participation. I wanted more than a sad, lonely ending to everything. I didn't want to be pitied in death.

I wanted the kind of completeness and unity you get from marriage. Instead of exchanging vows and rings, I would put my life in someone's hands, and they would unravel it, sweetly or cruelly. Pieces at a time or all at once. That's commitment, baby. The person who could do that would be death personified, as the lover that I had always wanted.

It was the mid-point of that second month as a murder bachelor when I got a message from Arthur. His screen name was *cafeskeleton*. For a while I called him Cafe as we progressed through messaging, emailing, then texting. That's when he said, *i think i should probably tell you my real name lol. if you want*

I replied, *careful ;) do you want me to have any identifying info . . . ?*

Arthur: *what are you gonna do when your head is in my freezer?*

I liked him. I asked if he was actually going to put my head in the freezer and he said *probably not, tbh, my freezer doesn't have a lot of room*. He had a real plan for disposing of my body, but he'd keep that to himself, until he knew I was for real.

We spent a lot of time feeling each other out. We talked for weeks, learning how serious we were. There was a constant "I'm just kidding!" vibe at first, contradicted by sincere insistence that this was what we were both looking for.

Anything we said otherwise was just being contrary for the sake of it, in case anything went wrong. "We were just kidding" was a flimsy legal defence, but in the hands of the right lawyer, it could be reinforced, right? We were cautious, building up to when we'd actually meet.

It was a kind of dance. It reminded me of secondary school with my boyfriend. We both knew we wanted to kiss, go out with each other, but teenagers were cruel and it wasn't unheard of to ask someone out then say, "Just kidding, it was a joke, I can't believe you took me seriously." This thing with Arthur was years later and far more significant, but it felt the same. I felt something, talking to him.

We organised our meeting over the phone. His voice was nice; a voice for late night radio, smooth and dark. He hummed and it buzzed against my ear. He asked, "You're not a copper, are you?"

I snorted. "You know that whole 'police can't lie to you' thing is rubbish, right?"

"Yeah, learning that broke my heart, along with 'if the teacher's not here after fifteen minutes we can go'." Fuck, he had a good laugh that made my toes curl to listen to. "Anyway, I dunno, figured I might catch you with your guard down."

Arthur wanted me to come to his place, and my first instinct was a very old one: *oh, I shouldn't do that, that's how people get murdered!* Then I remembered. The swell of laughter was delight, embarrassment and, oh, *excitement*, a feeling I'd been looking for forever. I told Arthur that I'd be there with bells on.

He lived a few hours away by train. Three and a half hours, exactly, complicated for an extra hour by leaves on the line. Then a forty-minute walk from the train station, to a cafe near his flat. He had wanted to meet me at the station but we agreed that wouldn't look good in court, if he didn't get away with killing me.

I called his name when I saw him. Arthur was tall and prematurely greying, pale-eyed with a scratchy-looking beard, big in a way that wasn't either fat or muscular. Sturdy, the way people are when they work physical labour. Looking at him made my stomach flip. I earnestly fancied him, but most of all I could see he was strong, and instead of thinking about how good he'd be at making me come I thought about how good he'd be at killing me. Strong hands, you know.

I wondered if he wanted to strangle me. We hadn't talked about how he was going to do it, only that he was going to, and that we were certain I wanted to die.

I hadn't been with anyone except my boyfriend, and he'd known me since he was a spotty teenage boy and I was an agonised teenage girl. Experiencing or acting on attraction to anyone else was as foreign as the empty land my body had become. I couldn't tell you if my hand fit poorly or well in Arthur's as he walked me to his flat.

Up four flights of stairs, no elevator. Running away from him would be difficult. That was exciting. That was the commitment I wanted. The flat was warm and dark, womblike with curtains drawn and the heating on. He took my jacket but didn't offer me a drink or anything to eat, instead leading me immediately to his sofa. We sat and talked and his fingers touched every stretch of bare skin that was on offer. My arms. The space between my jeans and the tops of my trainers. Collarbone, throat, jaw. I shifted in place and my shirt rode up, and he touched my stomach, fingers trailing above my belt.

I asked him, voice tremulous, "How are you going to do it?"

Arthur stilled, then slid his hand up my shirt. My breath caught. I don't know if either of us expected it to be like this, wanting over wanting, queer longing for several things at once, what we could give each other. He said, "I was going to pin you down and suffocate you."

The pitch of my voice shifted, becoming private and

wanting as his palm ran over my waist, up to my chest, calloused thumb prickling over my scars, my nipples. "Oh?"

"I got this see-through plastic bag," he told me, as he pulled my shirt up and off over my head. He kissed me, and put me on my back, used his hips to wedge my thighs apart. "It's in my bedroom." His voice was thin, wanting. "I didn't want to ruin you—"

"You can fuck me after," I offered, without thinking about it, overwhelmed and objectively thrilled by the idea of being something he would keep and want and have. I had a nice body. He should make good use of me, his reward for delivering me through death's pleasure into the dark. "When I'm still warm." He groaned and kissed me again, and I added, "And when I'm cold."

We'd never discussed it. I don't know if the idea had occurred to him before, but I could feel his excitement now. It took some visible restraint for him not to fuck me on the sofa, instead leading me to his bedroom. He'd clearly changed the sheets: they were pretty and pale and soft, and I wondered if he would nestle me into them, warm me up there. Looking at the floral pillows as he wrapped his arms around me from behind—his hand thumbing open my jeans and pressing inside them—made it all click into place: he wanted me to be his doll.

Flowery pink sheets were something that would've once triggered nauseous gender dysphoria in me. Here, it inexplicably looped itself all the way back round to gender euphoria. He was probably going to fuck me like a girl, but damned if I wasn't going to be the fucking prettiest corpse.

He undressed me like a real lover, excited to discover me for the first time. He worked slow and tender, mouth in soft places and on curves that I once resented for their shape. My boyfriend had always touched me kind of like a TV remote, something you pick up and know all the buttons by heart. He'd get me to the right channel and then enjoy his own movie.

Arthur, though; he was fascinated by me. He wanted to remember this, wanted to know the scars that ran over my chest, the geometric tattoo over my hip, the ways I was all man and "*so* beautiful," to him. He was going to miss me when I died, and there was a spark of smugness for that. He pinned me in place with those hands and I came *twice* before he even got the plastic bag out.

I wondered where he got it. I wasn't going to ruin the moment by asking, but it was big enough for a human head and clear enough to see through perfectly. Maybe it was an ultra-large food bag.

He put his weight beside me, opening the bag in his hands, and asked so tenderly that I wanted to cry: "Are you sure?"

I nodded. I felt like I was about to lose my virginity a second time. Fucking ridiculous. This wasn't even the first time I'd died, just the first time that I'd consented to it. I lifted my head so he could pull the plastic bag over my hair, over my face. I was already warm all over from fucking, and when I exhaled, the inside of the bag fogged up, my breath hot and wet across my face.

When I inhaled, the plastic weaved close, toxic and fume-like. Arthur's face was obscured. That loudness of death was creeping in, volume cranking up like a promise. I could hear the click of my own eyelashes, the rush of my heartbeat in my ears. It really did sound like the ocean. I could feel the ache where Arthur had been inside me with a keenness I never wanted to forget. The bag crinkled, pressing together as Arthur folded it at my neck. My pulse juddered against the tightening strips of plastic.

It wasn't tight enough that I couldn't breathe, yet. I wasn't being killed. I wasn't dying. This time, I knew *before* my body that I was going to die, and I wasn't bored by that prospect. I wanted it. I was starving for it. Hunger had been back and I hadn't realised; hunger had brought me here and let Arthur into my body, and hunger was going to let him take me out of it.

Fucking brilliant.

Arthur rolled me on my front without warning, winding me, and my instinctual gasp pulled the plastic tight, adhering it to my nose and mouth. The sudden lack of oxygen was *dizzying*. His weight pressed over my back, his knees were slung either side of me, pinning my arms in place. The sound of the plastic bag screamed in my ears as it pulled flat to every part of my face, tightened in Arthur's fist as his hand twisted, plastic cutting into my neck.

I was not a cow on a conveyor belt. I wasn't even a suicide with a gun. This was a real live murder that I wanted, that put slick heat back between my thighs. I don't know if it was pure lizard brain or if I started trying to breathe hard on purpose, but the loud noise of death became all-encompassing. I was making these hopeless sucking noises, struggling like a fish on land.

My eyes were rolling back in my skull. Arthur was hard again. Good for him. This was taking a while. I was choking on plastic, tasting it on my tongue, bile rising up in the back of my throat. My ears were getting tight. My throat felt cut off from everything, my tongue too big in my mouth. I was making noises like a pig being fucked.

Then, to my own disappointment, I passed out before I could die. I hadn't realised I would need it to be tailored, hadn't thought to ask Arthur to fix it so that I'd feel the moment of passage, where the big death would wipe out every little death. Instead, dark spots swarmed in front of my vision, and I thought, *fuck wait I wanted to be there when it happened* before consciousness collapsed in on me.

I landed softly in the void. The place I wanted to be. It felt like a ruined orgasm, though. I had been denied falling off the cliff. I screamed into the absolute nothingness.

And then I woke up. This time not in a mortuary, but sticky and bag-less and tucked into bed. Arthur was snoring next to me, facing away, the moon peering through a gap in the curtains, putting a long pale stripe over his bare shoulders. This wasn't fair. I started sobbing, ugly, resentful, no euphoria at life. Then Arthur woke up and started screaming.

I really thought death was going to stick this time. I hadn't considered coming back again as a possibility. I thought the first time had just been a fluke. If I knew I was going to wake up, I would've thrown myself in front of a train to scratch the itch sooner.

When we had both calmed down, I leaned against the wall, tears wiped away, frustration boiling as I listened to him sit on the bed and talk. "I made damn sure that you were dead," he said. "Your lips were blue, you'd thrown up on yourself, your eyes were all fucking bloodshot and glassy. I did it right. You were gone."

I wasn't covered in my own sick. Some of Arthur's come, but no vomit. I wondered if he had cleaned me up to kiss me. Touching to think about. But he kept talking, all fear and noise, asking how I could still be here, and it was draining. His fear didn't feel good. It wasn't bad, either. It was nothing. That stagnancy again. It was boring to watch Arthur be afraid of something that could be so good for him.

I was immortal. That was what I was realising. What he was yet to realise. I could be cut in half, turned into human smoothie in a plane engine, or fucked to death and I'd come back whole and unblemished. I could be a celebrity, a freakshow, a monster, anything I wanted. All I wanted was to die, and all Arthur needed was someone to die for him.

"*Fuck*, where are you going?"

I was walking out of his bedroom. Barefoot, buck arse naked, bullish. He stayed behind, and I knew he was listening with fear for the sound of his front door opening. I went to his kitchen instead. He had a beautiful set of knives in there. I didn't know how practical they were, but they had that folded steel look to them, waves in the metal like petrified wood.

Good, practical or even sharp didn't matter—not for what I wanted. I picked the longest carving knife and carried it back to the bedroom. Arthur had decided to quieten down and he was sitting on the edge of the bed, elbows dug into his knees, eyeing me warily, a hunter watching a wolf prowl. I stood in front of him and shivered happily when his eyes roamed over my body, to the places he'd already kissed and bitten and hurt. The things I felt for him—commitment, attraction—came back now that curiosity was returning to him.

"The first time I died," I told him, "I hardly lasted a day before I wanted to do it again. You'd be exactly the same. You'd kill me, then want to kill someone else. There's only so long you'd get away with it." I pressed the handle of the carving knife into his hand. "You want to kill and fuck whatever's left. I want to die, over and over. You've lucked out, Arthur, do you understand me?"

He looked so fucking doe-eyed as he nodded, but I knew he understood. I wasn't going to be his doll anymore. I'd give him plenty of ways to play with me, but I was going to be this man's God. I climbed into his lap, putting my hand between his legs, grasping where he'd gotten excited again. I put him inside me. There were a hundred thousand ways I could tell him to sacrifice at my altar. A hundred thousand ways to perfect death.

My knees clenched either side of his hips. The second offering he gave me was the knife: through flesh, up under my ribs, tickling my heart.

ABOUT THE AUTHORS

LC von Hessen is a writer of horror, weird fiction, and various unpleasantness, as well as a noise musician, multidisciplinary artist/performer, and former Morbid Anatomy Museum docent. Their work has appeared in such publications as *The Book of Queer Saints, Your Body is Not Your Body, Stories of the Eye, It Was All a Dream: An Anthology of Bad Horror Tropes Done Right*, multiple volumes of *Nightscript* and *Vastarien*, and the short ebook collection *Spiritus Ex Machina*. An ex-Midwesterner, von Hessen lives in Brooklyn with a talkative orange cat.

Theo Hendrie (he/him) is a horror-obsessed emo and writer of queer scary stories. He graduated with a Creative Writing (BA) from the University of Gloucestershire after a dissertation on transmasculine representation in horror. Find him making TikToks on his love of the genre or anywhere else on the internet as @theteddygutz.

Derek Des Anges is an emerging cross-genre trans author from London, UK. He's published works of cli-fi with *Other Worlds Ink* and *Parsec Ink*, and trans erotica with *New Smut Project*, among others. For future releases follow @derekdesanges on Twitter.

Winter Holmes is an author and illustrator from Maryland who is always on the lookout for the dark and strange. When they're not creating, they spend a lot of time with their oversized lapdog, Pippin. You can find them on Twitter and Instagram @winterholmesart.

gaast is a mess currently living on occupied Lenni Lenape land. It reads critical theory and writes speculative fiction. It was previously published in *Skulls and Spells*. Don't forget: Black Lives Matter.

Charles-Elizabeth Boyles is a contributing editor for Broken Hands Media. Their work has appeared in *E(i)dolon*, and pseudonymously elsewhere. They live in Kansas City, Missouri.

Hailey Piper is the Bram Stoker Award-winning author of *Queen of Teeth, No Gods for Drowning, The Worm and His Kings,* and other books of dark fiction. She is an active member of the Horror Writers Association, with dozens of short stories appearing in *Pseudopod*, *Vastarien*, *Cosmic Horror Monthly*, and other publications. She lives with her wife in Maryland, where their occult summonings are secret. Find Hailey at www.haileypiper.com, on Twitter as HaileyPiperSays, and elsewhere on social as haileypiperfights.

Joe Koch writes literary horror and surrealist trash. A Shirley Jackson Award finalist, Joe is the author of *The Wingspan of Severed Hands*, *The Couvade*, and *Convulsive*. Their short fiction appears in publications such as *Vastarien*, *Southwest Review*, *Pseudopod*, and *Children of the New Flesh*. He's been a flash fiction judge for Cemetery Gates Media and he recently co-edited the anthology *Stories of the Eye*. Find Joe (he/they) online at horrorsong.blog and on Twitter @horrorsong.

Layne Van Rensburg writes strange fiction for strange people (and non-people too). They live in the UK where they are studying for their PhD in mathematical biology. You can find them on Twitter @laynetheandroid or read more of their fiction at laynetheandroid.blogspot.com.

Bitter Karella is the writer and horror aficionado behind the microfiction comedy account @Midnight_pals, which asks what if all your favorite horror writers gathered around the campfire to tell scary stories. When not writing twitter jokes, she also dabbles in cartooning and text game design. His horror text games, available on itch.io, include *Night House*, *All Visitors Welcome,* and *Toadstools*.

Amanda M. Blake is a cat-loving daydreamer and mid-age goth who loves geekery of all sorts, from superheroes to horror movies, urban fantasy to unconventional romance. She's the author of horror titles such as *Nocturne* and *Deep Down* and the fairy tale mash-up series *Thorns*.

Lillian Boyd is a writer, editor, and musician who lives in California with her partners and cats. Bother her on Twitter at @herelieslill.

Taliesin Neith (he/they) was born in 1994, and grew up fascinated by all things morbid and grotesque. When he isn't daydreaming about monsters beyond human comprehension, they spend their time with their pet cats, playing video games, building keyboards, and working on digital art. He can be found on twitter @cadavertrial.

ABOUT THE EDITOR

Lor Gislason (they/them) is an autistic non-binary homebody from Vancouver Island, Canada. Their articles have been featured on Hear Us Scream, Horror Obsessive and several upcoming anthologies. Their dream is to one day make an encyclopedia covering body horror films.

Their novella, *Inside Out*, is available wherever goopy books are sold.

LIKE REAL | Shelly Lyons

ISBN: 978-1-943720-82-8 $16.95

This mind-bending body horror rom-com is a rollicking Cronenbergian gene splice of *Idle Hands* and *How to Lose a Guy in 10 Days*. It's freaky. It's fun. It's LIKE REAL.

XCRMNTMNTN | Andrew Hilbert

ISBN: 978-1-943720-81-1 $14.95

When a pile of shit from space lands near a renowned filmmaker's set, inspiration strikes. Take a journey up a cosmic mountain of excrement with the director and his film crew as they ascend into madness led only by their own vanity and obsession. This is a nightmare about creation. This is a dream about poop. This is a call to arms against vowels. This is *XCRMNTMNTN*.

BOUND IN FLESH | edited by Lor Gislason

ISBN: 978-1-943720-83-5 $16.95

Bound in Flesh: An Anthology of Trans Body Horror brings together 13 trans and non-binary writers, using horror to both explore the darkest depths of the genre and the boundaries of flesh. A disgusting good time for all! Featuring stories by Hailey Piper, Joe Koch, Bitter Karella, and others.

CONJURING THE WITCH | Jessica Leonard

ISBN: 978-1-943720-84-2 $16.95

Conjuring the Witch is a dark, haunted story about what those in power are willing to do to stay in power, and the sins we convince ourselves are forgivable.

WHAT HAPPENED WAS IMPOSSIBLE | E. F. Schraeder

ISBN: 978-1-943720-85-9 $14.95

Everyone knows the woman who escapes a massacre is a final girl, but who is the final boy? *What Happened Was Impossible* follows the life of Ida Wright, a man who knows how to capitalize on his childhood tragedies . . . even when he caused them.

THE ONLY SAFE PLACE LEFT IS THE DARK| Warren Wagner

ISBN: 978-1-943720-86-6 $14.95

In *The Only Safe Place Left is the Dark*, an HIV positive gay man must leave the relative safety of his cabin in the woods to brave the zombie apocalypse and find the medication he needs to stay alive.

THE SCREAMING CHILD| Scott Adlerberg

ISBN: 978-1-943720-87-3 $16.95

Scott Adlerberg's *The Screaming Child* is a mystery horror novel told by a grieving woman working on a book about an explorer who was murdered in a remote wilderness region, only to get caught up in a dangerous journey after hearing the distant screams from her own vanished child somewhere in the woods.

RAINBOW FILTH | Tim Meyer

ISBN: 978-1-943720-88-0 $14.95

Rainbow Filth is a weirdo horror novella about a small cult that believes a rare psychedelic substance can physically transport them to another universe.

LET THE WOODS KEEP OUR BODIES| E. M. Roy

ISBN: 978-1-943720-89-7 $16.95

The familiar becomes strange the longer you look at it. Leo Bates navigates a broken sense of reality, shattered memories, and a distrust of herself in order to find her girlfriend Tate and restore balance to their hometown of Eston—if such a thing ever existed to begin with.

SAINT GRIT| Kayli Scholz

ISBN: 978-1-943720-90-3 $14.95

One brooding summer, Nadine Boone pricks herself on a poisonous manchineel tree in the Florida backcountry. Upon self-orgasm, Nadine conjures a witch that she calls Saint Grit. Pitched as *Gummo* meets *The Craft*, Saint Grit grows inside of Nadine over three decades, wreaking repulsive havoc on a suspicious cast of characters in a small town known as Sugar Bends. Comes in Censored or Uncensored cover.

Ghoulish Books
PO Box 1104
Cibolo, TX 78108

☐ LIKE REAL	16.95
☐ XCRMNTMNTN	14.95
☐ BOUND IN FLESH	16.95
☐ CONJURING THE WITCH	16.95
☐ WHAT HAPPENED WAS IMPOSSIBLE	14.95
☐ THE ONLY SAFE PLACE LEFT IS THE DARK	14.95
☐ THE SCREAMING CHILD	16.95
☐ RAINBOW FILTH	14.95
☐ LET THE WOODS KEEP OUR BODIES	16.95
☐ SAINT GRIT Censored | Uncensored	14.95

Ship to:

Name ______________________________

Address ______________________________

City ____________________ State ________ Zip ________

Phone Number ______________________________

Book Total: $________

Shipping Total: $________

Grand Total: $________

Not all titles available for immediate shipping. All credit card purchases must be made online at GhoulishBooks.com. Shipping is 5.80 for one book and an additional dollar for each additional book. Contact us for international shipping prices. All checks and money orders should be made payable to Perpetual Motion Machine.

Patreon:
www.patreon.com/pmmpublishing

Website:
www.GhoulishBooks.com

Facebook:
www.facebook.com/GhoulishBooks

Twitter:
@GhoulishBooks

Instagram:
@GhoulishBookstore

Newsletter:
www.PMMPNews.com

Linktree:
linktr.ee/ghoulishbooks

Printed in the USA
CPSIA information can be obtained
at www.ICGtesting.com
LVHW031128011224
798045LV00047B/2183

* 9 7 8 1 9 4 3 7 2 0 8 3 5 *